For more than forty years,
Yearling has been the leading name
in classic and award-winning literature
for young readers.

Yearling books feature children's
favorite authors and characters,
providing dynamic stories of adventure,
humor, history, mystery, and fantasy.

Trust Yearling paperbacks to entertain,
inspire, and promote the love of reading
in all children.

OTHER YEARLING BOOKS YOU WILL ENJOY

THE MYSTERIES OF SPIDER KANE
Mary Pope Osborne

TOAD RAGE
Morris Gleitzman

CHITTY CHITTY BANG BANG
Ian Fleming

THE STORY OF DOCTOR DOLITTLE
Hugh Lofting

BLACK BEAUTY
Anna Sewell

I, HOUDINI
Lynne Reid Banks

THE UNSEEN
Zilpha Keatley Snyder

THE ROUNDHILL
Dick King-Smith

THE ISLANDER
Cynthia Rylant

THE CASTLE IN THE ATTIC
Elizabeth Winthrop

LITTLE FUR

A Mystery of Wolves

ISOBELLE CARMODY

A YEARLING BOOK

Text and illustrations copyright © 2007 by Isobelle Carmody

All rights reserved. Published in the United States by Yearling,
an imprint of Random House Children's Books, a division of Random House, Inc., New York.
Originally published in hardcover in Australia as
The Legend of Little Fur, Book 3, A Mystery of Wolves by Viking,
an imprint of Penguin Books Australia, Camberwell, in 2007.

Yearling and the jumping horse design are registered trademarks of Random House, Inc.

Visit us on the Web! www.randomhouse.com/kids

Educators and librarians, for a variety of teaching tools, visit us at
www.randomhouse.com/teachers

The Library of Congress has cataloged the hardcover edition of this work as follows:

Carmody, Isobelle.
A mystery of wolves / Isobelle Carmody.
p. cm. — (Little Fur ; bk. 3)
Summary: When Little Fur's feline friend Ginger goes missing, the tiny, half elf, half troll healer
undertakes an adventure that sets her on a collision course with a secret order of wolves.
ISBN 978-0-375-83858-3 (trade) — ISBN 978-0-375-93858-0 (lib. bdg.) —
ISBN 978-0-375-83859-0 (pbk.) — ISBN 978-0-375-84989-3 (e-book)
[1. Adventure and adventurers — Fiction. 2. Elves — Fiction. 3. Ecology — Fiction.
4. Animals — Fiction. 5. Magic — Fiction. 6. Fantasy.] I. Title.
PZ7.C2176My 2008
[Fic] — dc22
2007010922

Printed in the United States of America

10 9 8 7 6 5 4 3 2 1

First Yearling Edition

Adelaide

For Adelaide
my elf troll
my muse

CONTENTS

CHAPTER 1
A Herd of Dreams

Winter brings to the Land a mighty silence. Many beasts and birds fall deeply asleep under its spell, and the air turns thick with dreams.

Those who are wakeful can sense the chaotic power of these long, strange dreams. But only the creatures from the last age of the world know what is to be done with them. As the midwinter night approaches, they journey to one of the secret places where magic remains strong, and they enact the ancient ceremony of the Great

1

Weaving to summon the dreams and weave them into a potent gift for the earth spirit.

Only two kinds of creatures do not attend the midwinter weaving: trolls, who loathe the earth spirit with a deadly passion, and elves, for none survive in this age when magic is grown so thin.

Yet elf blood is not quite gone from the world, for there is one creature in whom it flows: a small elf troll named Little Fur.

Strangest of all the things of the last age she may be, for her father was an elf and her mother a troll. How this came about was not known, for Little Fur had no memory of her parents. She has lived her whole long life in a patch of wilderness that once lay at the heart of a vast forest of singing trees. Seven trees are all that remain, but these seven, known as the Old Ones, are saturated in the power of their fallen brethren. Though they sing no more, these sentinels protect the wilderness and all that dwell within it from the great dark human city that surrounds it.

Such is the power of the seven that even those humans who live alongside the wilderness never think of it.

Though it was still weeks away, Little Fur was already preparing for midwinter night with the help of the beasts and birds of the wilderness. The squirrels were so mad with excitement that even their usual scatterbrained usefulness evaporated. The birds who were willing forgot any instruction almost the moment it had been given. But the rabbits were steady as long as boldness was not required. The weasels and stoats were clever and nimble, and several older burrowers were hard at work making different sorts of hollows and nests for the visitors.

One afternoon Little Fur paused from the preparations to tend to a wild rabbit that had gotten her paw crushed by a branch. The wan sun was already setting as she carried the rabbit into a cave whose entrance was partly concealed beneath an icefall. This was where she made

and
stored
her potions
and herbs and did
much of her winter heal-
ing. Little Fur set the rabbit's
tiny bones and mended her torn skin.
Then she held her firmly as Tillet bandaged the
paw. Tillet, a large hare, was Little Fur's most
competent and steadfast helper.

"You have been brave," Little Fur whispered very softly, stroking the rabbit and looking around the cave.

The walls had niches of varying sizes that had been made by obliging moles. Many of the spaces

were filled with piles of leaves and packets of herbs and powders all carefully made up and labeled. Other niches were heaped with stones, dried roots, tubers and bags of seeds. One large niche held an abandoned beehive. Its honey had been drained into a gourd, but its wax was yet to be scraped out. Field mice slept in a nest in the niche beside the beehive; below, a recovering ermine lay curled asleep. Higher up were nests, several occupied by birds that had hurt their wings before they could fly away for winter.

The cave was warmer at the back because a trickle of hot springwater welled from a split rock and pooled in a natural stone bowl, where it shimmered with a strange blue light. Beside the stone bowl slept a blind tabby cat with three of her kittens. A fourth kitten swaggered in a circle beneath a cluster of bats suspended from a stalactite. Dangling beside the bats were a fat braid of garlic, strings of wild onions and three great, knotty, earth-encrusted roots. Toward the front of the cave, dried leaves and berries dangled from plaited reeds. Along a special shelf were small nut gourds containing Little Fur's more dangerous potions.

Though there were herbs waiting to be steeped and a great clump of spiderweb that needed weaving into bandages, Little Fur felt content. All these tasks could be dealt with after midwinter night. The one thing she ought to do before then was to make herself another cloak. The last one, sewn from a bit of human cloth, had fallen apart, and although Little Fur did not feel the cold as keenly as humans, she did need the cloak for all the pockets she could sew into it.

She sighed, remembering the gray cloak her elf father had left her. It could make its wearer hard to see and remained light as thistledown no matter what she put in the pockets. But a human had taken it the first time Little Fur had ever gone out into the city. All she had of her parents now was the green stone that had once belonged to her mother, which she wore on a thong about her neck. Little Fur had thought it merely a pretty bauble until she had learned that the stone was also worn by troll royalty.

Her longing to learn more of trolls was another reason that she looked forward to the coming midwinter ceremony. Little Fur had not thought much about her parents before traveling to the troll city of Underth, but that perilous adventure had awakened both her troll blood and a powerful curiosity. It was strange that the newly awakened troll blood was not constantly at war with her elf blood, but it was as if they had agreed that whichever served best would take charge.

"Finished," Tillet said.

Little Fur composed her mind and sang a song to the rabbit's spirit so the wounded paw could heal properly. A swan waiting to have his wings cleaned waddled nearer to listen, and a big beaver with a toothache ceased his restless movements. Once the rabbit was asleep, Little Fur lifted her gently into one of the ground-level niches.

An enormous black dog lay sprawled asleep against the wall with a small red snake coiled under her chest, a family of mice sleeping on her tail and a tiny owl perched on her back. The owlet opened her round yellow eyes and hooted a forlorn inquiry.

"Crow will come soon, Gem," Little Fur murmured, aware that the orphaned owl saw Crow as her brother, much to his disgust.

Crow was one of Little Fur's best friends, and their spirits were linked. This allowed her to sense that he was even now winging his way to the wilderness. She could feel that he had news, but that was nothing unusual. Crow loved to play messenger, and if the news was not exciting enough, he was happy to exaggerate it. Thinking about Crow turned Little Fur's mind to the cat Ginger. Her spirit was linked to his as well, but she had not seen him since they had been separated fleeing from Underth.

Little Fur began to examine the swan, grimacing at the sticky mess on his feathers. It smelled like the food that humans fed their road beasts, and she wondered how it had come to be in the pond. Fetching a bowl of water from the spring, she set it on the sand so that Tillet could pour in the frothy mixture she had prepared. The swan gave a hiss as he felt the warmth of the water, and Little Fur bade him be still, for the filth would not come off properly in cold water.

As she worked, her thoughts circled back to Ginger. He had taken the under-road from Underth, which went all the way to a distant city by the sea. The way back overland was much longer, for there were lakes and swamps and human settlements to avoid, as well as a high range of mountains to cross. With Ginger were a rat and two small ferrets, one of which had been injured, so that would have slowed him further.

Because of their connection, Little Fur could feel Ginger coming steadily closer each day. By her reckoning, he would arrive just before midwinter night.

Sorrow, the fox, would return then, too, or so he had promised when he'd left the wilderness the previous darkmoon. He had gone to the Sett Owl to ask her advice about a mate, only to be told there was no one for him and that he must learn to be wild.

Be patient, Little Fur told herself.

Little Fur sat back on her heels with weary satisfaction, seeing that the swan's feathers once again glowed white and clean. "Now you must preen out some oil," she told him. The swan thanked her and went to sit on a small puddle of meltwater, eyeing the dog mistrustfully. Little Fur was puzzled, for the swan knew that the earth magic that flowed through the wilderness would not allow the dog to attack any of Little Fur's patients.

Little Fur sniffed and was startled to find the

faint but unmistakable scent of human. The black dog had noticed as well. She had not been near a human since her escape from them. Now she stiffened and all the hair along her spine stood up as she rose, smelling of anger. The snake coiled himself more tightly, and the mice squeaked indignantly as they were spilled gently into the soft sand. Only the orphaned owlet clung to the dog's back with small thorny talons, her yellow eyes wide.

"What is the matter?" Little Fur asked.

The black dog loped past the meltwater pool and under the cluster of icicles at the mouth of the cave, the owl still clinging to her back.

Little Fur followed more slowly. Outside, the black dog was standing in the fresh snow as still as one of the great stones humans carved in their own likenesses. It was close to true darkness now, and there was a sharp blueness to the air.

Tillet bounded lightly outside, too. She stood up on her hind legs, long ears and nose twitching.

"Do you smell something?" Little Fur asked her.

The hare did not answer, but now her whiskers twitched as well.

"Something . . . ," Gem hooted softly from her

perch atop the black dog. "Definitely. Definably."

Little Fur was about to hush her nonsense when the black dog turned to look at her, eyes glowing ferociously. "I smell human."

Little Fur stared at her. "A human? But you don't . . . you can't mean that there is a *human* in the wilderness?"

The black dog gave a loud bark, bounded up the steep side of the valley and disappeared behind a line of fir trees cloaked in white.

CHAPTER 2
The Sick Human

The human had not so much invaded the wilderness as it had fainted and sprawled into it. Indeed, it was only the upper half of its body that lay within it. Nevertheless, Little Fur, the creatures who had followed her, the black dog and Tillet stared in disbelief.

"Is it a giant troll?" asked a small weasel.

"It is a human," said his sister, and the saying of it frightened her so much that she burst into tears.

"Is it an invasion?" asked her little brother,

half in terror, half in wonder. "Are they coming to kill us?"

"Sickness," said the black dog suddenly. The scent of anger she had given off shaded into something more complicated. Little Fur sniffed, and it was true: the scent of sickness rose unmistakably from the human.

"Bad sick," hooted Gem. "Sick of badness."

Little Fur went two steps closer, wondering what to do. She was not a healer of humans. Yet the wilderness had allowed this intrusion. No matter that the human had staggered here in a fevered daze, it would not have been able to enter had not the seven Old Ones permitted it. Did the trees wish her to heal the human? Or was it only an oddity caused by the long dreams of the birds and beasts caught up in winter's grip?

The black dog went closer to the human and nosed fearlessly at it.

Little Fur held her breath, half expecting it to wake and spring at her. But the human only moaned softly.

"It is in pain," she said, taking another step forward.

"Humans have their own healers," Tillet said firmly.

"We could pull it onto the black road. One of its own kind will see it soon enough," suggested a mink, glaring at the human with her shining black eyes.

Her mate nodded.

"It might be hurt by a road beast," Little Fur murmured. "They are the pets of humans, but I have heard many stories in which humans are mauled and killed by road beasts, just as animals and birds are."

"The human may be too sick

to be moved," suggested a tomcat who had come to find out what was happening.

Little Fur drew a long breath to steady herself and went to kneel beside the human. It was much bigger than she had expected, and its scent was so soured with despair that it smelled almost like a greep, one of the degenerate humans that in other seasons slept under trees and in holes and doorways throughout the city, stinking of the fermented juices they drank. Mingled with the reek of despair was the rotting stench of disappointment and the slick, sharp odor of helplessness. The human's body was weak with hunger and thirst, but the smells told Little Fur that its sickness lay in its spirit. It was rare to find a spirit that sickened while the body was sound. The last time she had smelled it had been in the fox Sorrow.

Little Fur gathered her courage and put out her hand to lay it on the human's bony wrist. Its pulse raced with fever and with the boiling

turmoil of its dreams, and she struggled for the
courage to merge spirits so that she could find the
song to heal it.

The human opened its eyes and looked straight
at her with eyes as blue as the summer sky, but it

did not see Little Fur. Indeed, its eyes fell closed almost at once. Little Fur knew that when it woke, it would think she had been a dream.

"What you are doing, Little Fur?" screeched Crow, landing in the snow beside her with a frenzied black flutter of his wings. "That being human! Must not touching it!"

"It is sick," Little Fur said.

"What that got to doing with Little Fur? You not healer of humanness!"

Little Fur ignored Crow and asked the black dog if she could drag the human around the wilderness and across the road to the pony park, where Brownie and his brothers lived with their human. Brownie was a small pony who visited Little Fur in the wilderness. He and his brothers gave rides to human children in the pony park in spring and summer.

The black dog said she could manage the task, and she twitched her back to dislodge the little owl. Gem fluttered to the ground with an enthusiasm that matched her awkwardness, landing

beak-first in a drift. Crow plucked her out and
set her upright.

"Heroic hero," Gem hooted adoringly.

"Stupidness," Crow muttered, hopping over to
Little Fur's side.

Little Fur bade him fly ahead to make sure there were no humans about. Crow gave a caw of irritation but launched himself into the air and followed the black dog. Gem gave a little hoot of wistfulness as Little Fur picked her up and set her onto a branch, her head swiveling to watch Crow.

"You really must learn to fly up soon, Gem. How will you ever get to know any other owls if you can't fly up to them?"

"I am crowful," said the owl soulfully.

Little Fur set off after the black dog, calling for Tillet to watch over the patients until she returned.

"Foolishness," the hare sighed under her breath.

❊   ❊   ❊

Brownie suggested that the black dog pull the human close to the front of his human's dwelling and then bark until the human came out. Little Fur observed from behind a bush as the black dog followed these instructions. She watched eagerly, as she had never seen Brownie's human before.

It was not long before the door of the dwelling opened and Brownie's human stepped out. It had gray and brown hair, which shone in the false light that poured out over its head and shoulders and lay glistening on the snow. Little Fur could not see the human's face because of the blinding glare of the false light, but she saw it stiffen when it saw the unconscious human and the black dog. It called out some words, and Little Fur smelled a question in them. Of course the sick human did not answer, but the black dog barked. Even though humans had almost no understanding of beast speech, Brownie's human seemed to get the sense of the black dog's barks.

It shouted something and then vanished inside.

Little Fur relaxed, for its words had smelled of concern and haste. A moment later, it came out wearing boots and a coat and carrying a blanket bundled up in its arms. It walked toward the unconscious human slowly, but its eyes were on the black dog. The human did not smell frightened, but its movements showed that it was wary. At last, it stood over the unconscious human, looking at the black dog. No words were spoken, yet it seemed to Little Fur that something passed between them.

Brownie's human bent to examine the sick human. The black dog watched for a time and then backed away. Noticing her retreat, Brownie's human called out. Little Fur could smell that the human had asked the black dog for help. She could hardly believe her eyes, but slowly the black dog retraced her steps.

Between them, Brownie's human and the black dog dragged the sick human toward the door. The black dog stopped at the edge of the dazzling spill of false light, and Brownie's human spoke

again, holding out one hand in entreaty. This
time the black dog gave a low warning growl and
showed her teeth before turning and loping

across the pony park to a border of fir trees that marched down one side in a line. Little Fur knew she had not gone toward the wilderness in case that made the human notice it.

The human murmured something that smelled of regret, then bent to pull the sick human the rest of the way into its dwelling. When the door closed behind them, Little Fur returned to Brownie, who was waiting agog to hear what had happened.

"I told you my human is kind," Brownie said triumphantly when Little Fur had told him everything.

Little Fur nodded, but she was thinking of the way the black dog had understood the human. Then she noticed something so very strange that it drove both the human and the black dog from her mind. Beside the door of the stable where Brownie and his brothers lived was a small fir tree draped with delicate glittering strands of material and hung with balls of shining colored ice, as well as the small shapes of deer and cats and other animals. At the highest point of the tree was a gleaming, pointed shape like a giant snow-flake.

"What has been done to the tree?" Little Fur asked, truly astonished.

"Humans always do that to trees in winter," Brownie said, seeming surprised at Little Fur's surprise.

"But . . . why?" Little Fur asked, amazed that she had never noticed this strange practice. But then she had never gone out of her wilderness in winter, for all of her planting of seeds in the city was done in spring and autumn.

"Humans being mad." Crow offered his opinion, perched on the stable door.

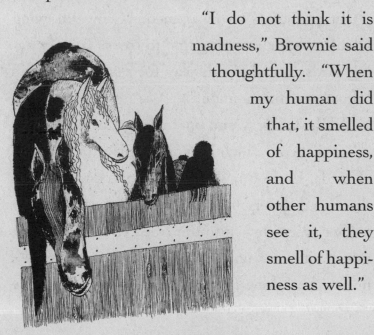

"I do not think it is madness," Brownie said thoughtfully. "When my human did that, it smelled of happiness, and when other humans see it, they smell of happiness as well."

"Perhaps it is winter that makes them do it," said Brownie's brother Sateen, putting his long nose over the wooden barrier. "Maybe it is to remind themselves of spring when the trees come into blossom. Maybe that bright thing at the top is meant to be a sun."

"I think the winter makes humans feel the flow of earth magic, and so they worship it," Brownie said. "That is why they put a big snowflake on top."

"Stupidness," Crow opined. "Crow knowing what for humans doing that to trees. They copying birds to making display for mate. Brownie's human wanting a mate."

While Crow went on to boast of the many other ways in which humans copied the wisdom of birds, Little Fur went to the tree and reached through its finery to touch the knobby trunk. She let her spirit flow into the tree's dream. Though asleep, it was dimly aware of what Brownie's human had done to it, and not displeased. Little

Fur found a memory of the human, touching its branches gently and singing.

Singing!

Little Fur's toes prickled with excitement, because the beaked house was full of a still magic brought there unwittingly by humans when they came to sing and yearn. Was this garbing of trees another sort of magic?

That night the black dog had not yet returned to the wilderness. Little Fur lay curled in a soft nest in the roots of the eldest of the ancient trees. She told herself that even if the black dog was roaming the city streets, she had the means to protect herself.

But what if staying away from the wilderness was not the black dog's idea? What if she had been taken captive? Little Fur knew that humans captured cats and dogs in the street, and if humans did not come for them, they were killed. No one knew why.

Little Fur sighed and let her spirit sink into the tree's spirit, deciding that on the morrow, she would ask Crow to see if he could find the black dog if she had not yet returned.

She slept.

CHAPTER 3
A Song of Hope

Little Fur dreamed.

It was a dream not of pictures, but of feelings and smells. It began with a thick black reek that reminded her of the sticky stuff on the swan's feathers. Then she felt a terrible sharp pain in her hand, as if someone had thrust a thorn deeply into it. The pain shifted into her chest and became a flabby gnawing pain, which stretched out until she realized it was the link between her and Crow and the gray cat. It was pulling, hurting her.

Then she saw Ginger. He was backed against a stone wall, his fur matted and filthy. His eyes shone with a ferocious light she had never seen in them.

Let me go, he snarled.

Little Fur woke.

It was not yet dawn, and the air was still and very cold. She pressed her face against the thick roots of the Old One until her heart ceased galloping. Then she sat up and rubbed a dusting of snow from her cheeks, telling herself the bad dream had come from touching a human, and from her worry that the black dog had been captured by humans. Ginger was not in danger. He was coming home. Hadn't she been feeling that for many days now?

But as she rose and padded out into the blue black morning, she rubbed at her chest and shivered.

The sky was very clear, and the few stars remaining sparkled like chips of ice. The pale

winter sun rose just as she reached the hill
meadow and took the path winding down from it
to the tumble of black boulders at the base of the

icefall. The sun made the great cluster of ice glitter rose pink.

Inside the cave, Tillet looked up in mild surprise, for usually Little Fur did not come until later. But the hare merely pointed to a bowl of oil filled with leaves. Little Fur checked the leaves, then went over to the bench and began to assemble the ingredients for a bone-setting potion. Tillet was making a mash that dwarfs liked. They worked companionably in silence until Crow skimmed under the icefall, over the sleeping swan, to land on a branch beside Gem. The little owl fluffed her feathers and gazed in adoration at Crow, who ignored her.

"Crow dying," he announced mournfully. "Crow having heart attacking maybe."

Little Fur felt a small flutter run through her. "Did you dream, Crow?"

"Crow dreaming and snow dreaming," Gem chanted.

"Hush, Gem," Little Fur said. "Crow, did you dream about Ginger last night?"

Crow stared at her with his yellow eyes and gave an uneasy croak.

"Oh, Crow! I dreamed of him, too! I dreamed that he is in danger. It hurt me, too."

"Gem dreaming danger," Gem hooted.

"Copying," Crow sneered.

Little Fur was not so sure. Ginger was the one who had rescued the owlet when her egg had been blown from her nest and cracked open. The gray cat had carried the tiny featherless creature in his mouth from the city to the wilderness, which meant he was the first creature Gem had touched and smelled. That meant he had probably evoked the mother bond in the little owl, and there was power in that.

"I tried to feel where Ginger is this

morning, but there are too many dreams in the air," Little Fur murmured.

"After midwinter . . . ," Crow began.

"No," Little Fur said. "I must go and see the Sett Owl now."

"No usefulness in going to Sett Owl," Crow said. He preened, then announced in the somber voice he kept for serious messages that the Sett Owl was very ill and seeing no one.

"Then I must go and see if I can help her," Little Fur said at once. "Do you know what is wrong with her?" She knew that Crow could not have spoken to the Sett Owl himself. The old bird never allowed any crows to enter the beaked house because she had been crippled by crows.

Crow clacked his beak sullenly. "Squirrels tell that Sett Owl leaking," he finally said.

Little Fur spent the rest of the morning making the tediously difficult bone-setting potion she had begun. There were many ingredients, which had to be added in certain specific amounts and in a careful order. She had chosen this task deliberately, for aside from its being one of her important winter jobs, Little Fur had known that the making of it would consume all of her attention and stop her worrying.

By the time the potion was complete, it was midafternoon. Little Fur was going to wait until the sun set, but Crow told her that the whole city was shrouded in a thick, damp fog and there was not a human or a road beast to be seen anywhere. This meant she would be a lot safer than when she ventured out on her seed-planting expeditions.

There was no sign of the fog outside the cave, but the weather in the wilderness often differed from the weather in the surrounding city. Bidding farewell to Tillet and all those patients who were awake, Little Fur lifted Gem onto her shoulder and set out.

When she got to the edge of the wilderness, she saw that the world beyond was indeed swathed in a dense white. It was only a mist, and yet when she stepped out of the protective embrace of the wilderness, she felt a plucking at her hair and a prickliness brushing at her cheeks. It was the winter dreams. Little Fur was glad of Gem's small warm weight on her shoulder and the soft prick of her tiny talons.

Little Fur had made up her mind that even if Gem was not dreaming of Ginger, it was time she learned to be a proper owl. None of the owls had accepted the small orphan into their nests when Little Fur had last brought her to the Sett Owl as a lost chick, but surely Gem was not to be banned from owldom forever because of an accident of the wind! How was she to learn what it was to be an owl unless she was able to be around other owls!

Little Fur reached the human dwellings bordering the field that led away from the wilderness, and she entered the snowy lane between them. In spring, she could hear the muffled voices of humans, as well as the chatter of birds, the hum of insects and the occasional distant roaring of a road beast. But now there was utter silence save for the soft squeak and puff of snow under her feet.

At the end of the lane, she stopped and gaped to see that the great black roads that lay beyond had almost vanished under a thick pelt of snow. Usually in winter, the snow on a road was soon stained black. There must have been a fresh fall during the night, and no road beast had passed yet.

Being part troll, Little Fur must never lose touch with the earth, growing things or water, lest she be severed from the flow of earth magic forever. Little Fur put her foot gingerly onto the snow and found that, like the smaller black roads

that ran by the wilderness, it had earth magic flowing over it. That meant that for the first time, she would not have to crawl through one of the pipes that ran under the road. She would simply be able to walk across it.

"What you waiting for?" Crow screeched impatiently from overhead.

Little Fur took a breath and stepped onto the road. Soon she had crossed all three roads and was making her way along the high wooden barrier that Brownie called a fence. She had never learned the purpose of these fences humans built, and she sometimes suspected that Crow was right in saying that humans did not know why they built them.

The mist ahead was flooded with false light, which meant she had almost reached the beast feeding place. Soon she came to the place where the fence angled away from the road and around the back of the feeding place. It was a dwelling made entirely of the humans' unmelting ice. A glaring flood of false light flowed into the darkness in all directions. Little Fur had learned that road beasts would not attack unless you walked on a black road in front of them. But there were no road beasts now taking shelter under the great stiff wings of the feeding place.

There was a strange beauty to this dwelling, yet it reeked of the awful liquid fed to road beasts. Crow flapped into her face to ask crossly why she was standing still as if she were hoping to cast roots. Little Fur brought her mind back to the moment. "Can you find the black dog?" she asked Crow.

Crow reluctantly nodded, knowing he would not be

welcome at the beaked house, and flew off into the mist.

Little Fur hurried around the fence to the crooked board. She slipped through the gap into the field behind it. Then she stopped and stared — for what had been a wasteland full of poisonous dead patches was transformed by the snow into a pristine plain.

Little Fur crossed it, noting with pleasure the crisscrossing tracks of rabbits, hares, foxes, birds and deer; then she came to the stand of pear trees. She touched one, closing her eyes and letting her spirit go into its wood and into its dream. She saw the six tiny pear trees that had sprung from seeds she had taken from it and that stood close by the Old Ones, flooded with golden autumn light, their branches heavy with yellow pears.

A bell began to toll. It was the bell that hung in the pointed roof of the beaked house, which lay across another snowy field and over a hedgerow. The bell was still ringing as she crawled

under the black branches of the great thorny
hedgerow and climbed to her feet. She stared in
astonishment at the great flock of humans standing in the yard of the beaked house, many bearing

candles that shone a soft warmth onto their cheeks and eyes!

Then the humans began to sing.

Little Fur had felt the power of human song before, but she had never heard so *many* humans singing together, nor had the songs ever been such an outpouring of hope and longing. The music was so beautiful and potent that she felt dizzy with wonder. She crept to the barrier of spiked metal poles driven into the earth, which served as a fence for the beaked house, wanting to see if she could smell what had caused this gathering.

But even as she reached the fence, the song ended and the bell ceased to ring. The humans began to laugh and talk and break up into small groups that moved gradually down the path away from the beaked house. Somewhere she heard the sounds of road beasts groaning and growling reluctantly to life. Behind, on the snow-covered cobblestones, she now saw a grouping of large stone carvings that she had not seen before.

After the two black-clad humans that cared for the beaked house had gone away down the path, Little Fur slipped between the spikes and went to look more closely at the carvings.

The stone forms had been arranged facing a she-human carving nursing its youngling. Several of the stone watchers were even beast-shaped! Then Little Fur saw with astonishment that the great tree alongside the beaked house was draped with shimmering strings and glittering bubbles and icicles in a rainbow of colors, just like the little fir tree in Brownie's stable yard!

She felt suddenly sure that what had been done to the trees was connected to the singing of the humans. Hadn't Brownie said that his human sang as it draped the tree with finery?

She was about to go to the opening at the base of the wall, which beasts and other creatures lacking wings used to enter the beaked house, when she heard a voice call her name. Puzzled, but unable to see who had spoken, Little Fur went around to the front of the beaked house,

47

where wide steps led up to the doors that humans used to enter. The doors stood ajar. A golden light poured through the gap and lay in a bright strip on the snow.

A tiny black form standing in the light beckoned to her.

CHAPTER 4

A Mystery of Wolves

"The Sett Owl is expecting you," Indyk the monkey said when Little Fur got to the top of the snowy steps.

Little Fur was not surprised that the Sett Owl knew she had come—nor that another creature had taken up Gazrak's duties as caretaker, since the faithful rat, like Ginger, had yet to return from Underth. The Sett Owl was a seer, after all, and saw many things with the help of the still magic of the beaked house.

The monkey beckoned to Little Fur again. She stepped through the great oak doors into the still magic. Little Fur was reassured to feel the earth magic flowing through the floor so that she would not lose touch with it. Her ears tingled slightly as the still magic pressed and nuzzled at her affectionately, as if it remembered her from other visits. She had to force herself to pay attention as Indyk explained that the doors of the beaked house were left open two nights in the whole turn of seasons, and tonight was one of them.

"Why?" Little Fur asked curiously.

The monkey frowned and shook his head. "The Sett Owl did not say."

"I heard that she was ill," Little Fur said as they entered the vast main chamber of the beaked house with its high, intricate curved roof. The enormous stone giants set about the walls gazed down at her, their expressions as sorrowful as ever.

"The Sett Owl is very ill," Indyk said.

50

"I have brought my healing pouches," Little Fur said stoutly.

"I do not think they will help, Healer," Indyk said.

"Why doesn't the still magic heal her?" Little Fur asked.

"She is like a vessel that is very old and worn, and yet she must contain all of the strange, heavy power of this house. She says one will come who is to take her place. I think it is only wishfulness. Come—she is awake, and you will be able to speak with her."

He took Little Fur to a window ledge. In the deep shadows perched the Sett Owl. A piece of white cloth lay crumpled behind her, and Indyk tut-tutted as he leaped nimbly to drape it about the Sett Owl, taking particular care with a wing that seemed stiff and uncomfortable.

"Do not fuss, Indyk," said the owl.

"It is my business to fuss, just as it is your task to endure my fussing," Indyk said, tucking the cloth in to keep it secure. His brisk kindness reminded Little Fur of Tillet. He leaped down and told Little Fur, "Do not interrupt when she talks. It tires her enough to speak without having to repeat things constantly. It is amazing how few creatures can listen."

"He is right about one thing," the Sett Owl said, swiveling her head to look down at Little Fur. "I am tired."

After a long moment, Little Fur said timidly, "I will make you a tisane for your wing."

The owl gave a dry croak of laughter. "Why not? The flavor of kindness is sweet."

"I have brought many other herbs and potions with me." Little Fur took Gem and set her down, then removed her healing pouches.

"You have brought what I need," the owl said. "But it is not ready."

"It will not take me long to mix something if you will tell me what is wrong. Do you have a fever?"

"I am fevered with impatience," the owl said, and sighed. "Ask your questions."

"I . . . I do not want to disturb you," Little Fur said. "But I have dreamed that Ginger is in danger. Crow dreamed it, too. I want to know if the dream is true."

"A crow does not dream true," the owl echoed coldly.

"Brother Crow," Gem hooted, so loudly that Little Fur jumped.

"Brother!" the Sett Owl hooted with her dry laughter. "Should an owl call a crow brother?"

"Beloved brother," Gem hooted defiantly, but she was trembling.

"Can you tell me if Ginger is in danger?" Little Fur asked the Sett Owl.

The owl's eyes grew cloudy. Little Fur felt the still magic thicken. "He is."

"What is the danger? Where is he?" Little Fur asked.

"If you would find the cat, you must seek out the Mystery of Wolves."

Little Fur stared at the owl. "Do you mean that wolves have taken Ginger captive? And what of the others? Gazrak and the ferrets?"

"Seek the Mystery of Wolves, and you will have the answers to the questions you ask and to the questions you do not ask," the owl said. She turned her eyes to where Gem stood. "Take the owlet."

"Sett Owl, please. I brought her here only because I hoped you would appoint someone to teach her how to be a proper owl."

"She is a fallen owl," the Sett Owl said. "No one can teach her what she needs to know. She must find the courage to fly up to what she can be. She has some bravery, if she would call a crow 'beloved,' but her head is empty. Take her with you, and she may gain wisdom."

"Take her where?" Little Fur asked.

But the Sett Owl had closed her eyes.

"I am afraid she will sleep for a long time now,"

Indyk said apologetically. He set down the bowl of water he had brought and leaped up to replace the white cloth, which had slipped from the sleeping owl. Leaping back onto the floor, Indyk said, "If you mix the tisane, I will give it to her when she wakes."

Little Fur carried Gem to a place where she could work, and then she mixed the tisane. When it was complete, Little Fur admitted to Indyk that she had not understood what the owl had told her. "Perhaps I should wait until she wakes and ask her to explain," she said.

"She does not often wake now," Indyk replied cautiously.

Little Fur nodded sadly and handed him the

tisane. Then she packed away her herbs and restored Gem to her shoulder. By then the monkey was nowhere to be seen, so Little Fur left an offering of some dried plums and went back outside. To her surprise, she found Sly the cat sitting curled on the front step of the church, grooming one elegant black paw.

"Greetings, Little Fur," Sly purred, rising gracefully. "Crow told me about Ginger, so I came to see what the Sett Owl advised."

Little Fur stroked the cat's sleek back, and

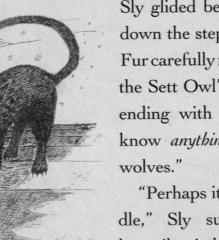

Sly glided beside her down the steps. Little Fur carefully repeated the Sett Owl's words, ending with "I don't know *anything* about wolves."

"Perhaps it is a riddle," Sly suggested, her tail twitching with interest.

"What is a riddle?" Little Fur asked. She had wondered at the word before.

"A riddle is a puzzle," Sly said. "A thing to be solved."

"A riddle is a mystery, but not all mysteries are riddles," Gem hooted softly.

"Have you a bird nesting in your hair now?" Sly asked, her single green eye glinting with laughter. "Have you run out of trees to store your patients in?"

"She is the orphaned owl whose life Ginger saved. I think she has been dreaming of Ginger, too, but it is hard to tell," Little Fur said. "She is too young to know what she says most of the time."

"Some say that the greatest wisdom is hidden inside a nut of foolishness. The trick is how to crack it open," Sly said.

At that moment, Crow swooped down from the sky to land on one of the stone shapes. He had not found anyone who had seen the black dog, he announced. Little Fur thanked him and

again repeated what the Sett Owl told her.

"Wolves eating birds and small creatures," Crow said. "That being their dangerfulness."

"Wolves do not come into human cities," the cat said. "If you want to find them, you will have to go out into the great wilderness."

"One wolf is being in the citydom," Crow said. "He is captivated in the zoo. Maybe that being what owl meaning."

"Zoo," Sly murmured, giving off the hot, strong scent of her curiosity. "I have heard of zoo. Let us go there now."

"It is on the other side of the city," Little Fur protested.

"It is snowing," Sly said carelessly. "Perhaps this wolf will tell you what you need in order to understand the owl's advice."

Little Fur found herself reluctantly agreeing, and off they set.

An hour later, Crow swooped down to tell Little Fur that the zoo was just ahead. In a few moments, she was gazing up in dismay at a high stone wall that ran away into the mist in either direction.

"Following the wallness," Crow cawed from above.

Little Fur and Sly did as he suggested. They soon came to a high gate in the wall made of thick strands of twisted metal. Beyond it, a snowy path wound neatly away through a hedge that had been trimmed to have the squared lines of a wall. The top of the hedge was white with snow. There was no one inside, so Little Fur pushed through a gap in the metal strands. As she waited for Sly to come through, she sniffed. Her eyes widened at the multitude of unknown scents. Then Sly was beside her, single green eye glittering, long, elegant black tail lashing backward and forward.

CHAPTER 5
The Zoo

"Crow will flying to find the wolf," Crow said.

Little Fur watched him flap away, then turned to Sly. The cat's tail was disappearing around a bush farther down the path. Little Fur went after her and found a smaller path curving away from the main path. She nearly called out to Sly, but there was something unnatural about the mingling of so many smells, and it made her reluctant to shout. So she just followed her past numerous enclosures filled with strange animals. She wished she had time to stop, but Sly's speed reminded her of the urgency of their journey.

Little Fur caught up with Sly at an enclosure with a fence so low that Sly leaped over it and sniffed at the bases of several dead trees. In the branches above sat a number of small black-eyed animals with large, soft, fur-tipped ears and long, lustrous ringed tails. They gazed down at Sly, who studied the dangling tails before leaping onto a snowy bench and grooming herself.

"What kind of beast are you?" Little Fur asked one of the animals, wondering why Sly had stopped here.

"We are lemurs," said the biggest of the creatures. "That is what the humans call us. My name is Orin. Why have *you* come here?"

"I came to speak with the wolf," Little Fur said.

All the black-eyed lemurs cast startled looks at a small, rather unkempt member of their clan. This one bared his teeth and lifted his tail to throw it about his neck. For a moment, he looked very fine and dignified; then he forgot himself and began to gnaw at the end of his tail.

"You are the elf troll who saved the trees from the tree-burning humans and who traveled to Underth to battle the Troll King?" Orin asked Little Fur.

"I did not battle the Troll King," Little Fur said. "But I did go to Underth. How did you know?"

"*He* dreamed that the elf troll who did those things would come in search of a wolf," Orin said, flicking a dismissive look at the tail-gnawing lemur. "His name is Ofred, and he sometimes dreams true things."

"Sometimes! Oh, sometimes!" Ofred hissed. He burst into wild laughter that made the hair stand up on Little Fur's neck and toes.

"I am Little Fur," she said. "Is it true that you dreamed of me coming here?"

"Impossible things can be done only by impossible creatures," Ofred said. "Here is a riddle. How can an elf love a troll?"

"I do not know," Little Fur said.

"The elf troll will lose her way. The darkness will devour her unless she can find the deepest green. If she does not find it, the world itself will fall to darkness. So said the wizard who was of the first age of the world and the last of her kind." The lemur gave another mad cackle of laughter.

"What you are doing here?" Crow cawed,

coming to land on the low fence. "Wolf not being here. Coming!"

Little Fur bade the lemur clan farewell and continued along the path. "That fence was so low," she said to Sly. "They could all escape if they wanted to."

"That is why they have no need," Sly said.

"Here being wolf," Crow cawed, landing on the path just ahead.

Little Fur joined him and looked into the cage. An old wolf lay on a rock. He lifted his head, and his eyes shone with a fierce, sad pride.

"Greetings, Wolf. I am Little Fur, and I have come to ask you a question," Little Fur said.

"You smell of troll," rasped the wolf.

"I am an elf troll," said Little Fur. "Do you know of the Sett Owl?"

"I have heard of her," answered the wolf.

"I dreamed of a friend in danger. The Sett Owl said the dream was true, and that if I would save him, I must discover the Mystery of Wolves."

The wolf rose with a swift grace that belied the gray fur around his muzzle. "What has the Mystery of Wolves to do with your friend?"

"I do not know. My friend is a cat and he was journeying here from the city by the sea with three smaller animals. Perhaps wolves took them captive."

"Wolves do not take captives," said the old wolf with austere dignity. "That is a human thing. If your friend did some harm to a member of the pack, he would have been killed."

Little Fur drew close to the bars. "Can you tell me

what the Mystery of Wolves is? Is it a secret?"

"It is not a secret," said the wolf. "The Mystery of Wolves is an order of mystic wolves that dwells in the mountains."

Little Fur stared into the wolf's pale blue eyes. "An order?"

"It is a pack led by a dream," said the old wolf.

"Where do lost dreams lead?" Gem hooted softly.

"Where is the home of the pack?" Little Fur asked.

"It is in the mountains that lie between this city and the sea. If you free me, I will lead you to the Mystery," the old wolf said.

Little Fur looked at the strong bars of the cage and the heavy lock on its door. "I am sorry, but the bars are too thick and the lock is too strong," she said. "I am only a healer."

The wolf turned away.

"I think you will need the wolf's help if you are to find Ginger," Sly said with a little hiss.

Little Fur flinched as the thorny talons of the little owl under her hair sank in, reminding her that the Sett Owl had told her to take Gem with her. She took another look at the wolf's cage, hoping an idea would come to her.

"Excuse me," said a deep, rich voice. "Did I hear you say that you wanted a cage opened?"

Little Fur looked to see a vulture sitting on a perch in an open enclosure. She had a metal ring on her leg, and a chain ran from it to another ring set into the side of her perch.

"There are keys to all of the cages in the office of the human keepers. They hang on a great circle on a hook. I know exactly where it is. You see that green building near the wall? There is a window that stays open where birds and beasts are sometimes brought if they are ill. Only free me. It will not be hard. The chain on my leg ends in a pin that is through the ring in my perch. I cannot get it out with beak or claw, but your fingers are clever, like those of a human. Help me and I will help you."

"Never trusting a vulture," Crow croaked.

"That is a harsh thing to say," the vulture said reproachfully. "Will you refuse me, Healer? Is not the bestowing of freedom an act of healing?"

"I don't know," Little Fur said. "It might be."

"Then free me. Do not fear my sharp beak. Never would I be so craven as to peck the hand that freed me." She shifted to the end of her perch and pecked fretfully at the chain.

Little Fur made up her mind. She entered the vulture's enclosure and began to work the pin out. The moment it fell free, the vulture spread her wings and rose into the air.

"So much for that," Crow said.

"I am sorry to have tricked you," the vulture called. "I am too big to get through the window, but a smaller bird might manage it."

"It bound to being a trap!" Crow said in a sinister voice. But when Little Fur said nothing, Crow put on a martyred look and flapped away, calling dolefully, "Nevermore."

Sly had gone along the path and was looking

into another enclosure. Little Fur was about to
call her back when she noticed how rigidly the

black cat stood. Her long, narrow tail was fluffed all along its length. It was so unlike her that Little Fur went to see what she had found.

She gasped at the giant cat behind the bars, stretched out with savage elegance. His fierce, tawny eyes were locked on Sly. His fur was black as night, black as blackest shadow.

"How dared they to have caged you?" Sly said. There was something in her voice that

Little Fur had never smelled before. Sly padded closer to the bars, trembling from head to toe.

"Humans dare any-thing in their ignorance. I was much smaller when they captured me. Indeed, it was so long ago, I do not remember it."

"You must be freed," Sly said passionately.

"Will you free me? I promise you that I will kill the moment I am free. I will kill and kill and kill until my rage is sated." The enormous black cat yawned, baring fangs.

"I would free you," whispered Sly.

He eyed her with ferocious amusement. "My name is Danger, emerald eye. I will kill you if you free me."

"I will free you," Sly vowed.

Danger stared into her eyes. Then he yawned again. "Will you bite through the bars with your terrible fangs? Will you tear open the lock with your savage claws?" There was mockery in his voice, and Sly flinched as if he had slashed at her with his claws.

"There are keys."

"The key to my cage is kept on a chain around the neck of the she-human who rules this place," said Danger. "No one ever comes into my cage but that one. It calls me Beauty and whispers its dreams to me. One day I will lure it close enough to teach it my true name."

Crow was overhead now, squawking. Little Fur turned to see him descend with a shining circle hung with many keys. "Hurrying," Crow cawed, panting from his exertions. "Soon humans coming."

Sly sniffed at the keys, but Little Fur could see

already that they were all too small for the great lock on the door of the giant cat's cage.

"Lucky for you, emerald eye. Run far and fast before my teeth close on your throat," said the great black cat. He gave a terrible snarling growl of laughter and rage.

"A true thing, caged, does not know itself," Gem hooted softly.

Sly said nothing as they returned to the cage of the wolf.

Little Fur unlocked the door, and the old wolf leaped out onto the snow. "We must go at once," he said. "I must be far from this place before the humans find my empty cage."

The wolf padded along the trail they had left in the snow. In a moment, they were at the front gates to the zoo. Little Fur was dismayed to find that the wolf was too big to fit between the bars.

"I will hide in the bushes, and as soon as the gates are opened, I will come out," the wolf said decisively. "You must go, and I will find you."

"I do not know the way," Little Fur reminded him.

"Go that way," he said, pointing in the direction opposite of the wilderness. "To the mountains. Go as fast as you can."

Little Fur nodded, and then she saw that Sly had not come through the gate.

"I will stay here," Sly said. Little Fur had never seen the black cat so solemn. Suddenly she was afraid for her, for what had kept the cat safe all her dangerous life was her pure detachment. But now she smelled of caring.

"He will not spare you out of gratitude if you free him," Little Fur said. "He is too wild for that."

"I do not want his gratitude," Sly said. "I want him to be free."

"There is no time for this," barked the wolf. "Go! I will find you soon." He bounded away.

Little Fur gave Sly a pleading look, but the one-eyed cat turned and stalked away. Little Fur looked up to where Crow was wheeling in the sky.

"Go, go," urged Gem on her shoulder.

Little Fur gathered her courage around her and squeezed back through the fence.

She did not look back.

CHAPTER 6
Graysong

"He will not coming," Crow cawed as Little Fur began walking. "He will being caught."

Little Fur said nothing, for it seemed all too likely that the old wolf *would* be caught. Yet there was nothing to be done but to go in the direction of the mountains and hope. Little Fur headed along a street where many road beasts slept under heavy pelts of snow.

The street led to a great open space, in the center of which was yet another fir tree that had been hung with jewels and strands of glittering silver and gold. When Little Fur reached the tree, the mist was so thick that she could no longer see the human dwellings about the edges of the open space. She could have been standing in the midst of a vast snowy plain, and very soon she might be doing exactly that.

Crow flapped down to tell her that she must hide, because some humans were coming. Since

there was no shelter except the tree, Little Fur slipped under its resinous branches and pressed herself against its trunk. Gem gave a soft hoot of fear, and Little Fur stroked her downy feathers. The humans stopped at the tree. Little Fur smelled the pleasure the sight of it gave them. Then they passed on and out of hearing.

"Coming out now," Crow cawed from above.

Little Fur emerged warily, and as she did, the wolf appeared out of the mist.

"The humans chased me," he said without a hint of fear, "but I lost them. I have smelled a way for us to go out of the city."

Little Fur smiled and said, "I am ready."

"Ready, too," hooted Gem.

The wolf led them across the open space and down a narrow lane, which brought them to one of the older parts of the city with many empty dwellings, half crumbled down. Usually such places were dangerous, because greeps lived there and many troll holes opened into them. But now all was white and silent.

They came to a bridge, and instead of going across it, the wolf went under it. The bridge spanned a steep-sided channel along which ran two shining metal rails. Little Fur knew that road serpents used the rails, but that for all the terrifying racket they made, they would not cause harm so long as you did not get in their way.

"This way?" Little Fur asked, her voice strong.

"You are brave," the wolf said approvingly. "That is fortunate."

He leaped down into the channel. Little Fur climbed down carefully after him. They passed under two bridges, and as they were approaching the third, Little Fur heard human voices. Before any of the humans saw them, Crow flapped overhead, cawing loudly to draw their attention. Little Fur was very relieved when the channel angled down into the earth and became a tunnel.

"You smell of troll even more now," the wolf said after they had been going down for a time.

"It is my troll blood," Little Fur explained. "When I am under the earth, it grows stronger than my elf blood."

The wolf told her his name was Graysong, and

asked where she had come from. She told him of
the wilderness, then she asked how he had come
to be in the zoo.

"I was caught in a human trap," Graysong said. "I had been driven from my pack after a challenge. I had not yet learned how to be a lone wolf."

"Do you know any of the wolves of the Mystery?"

"Their leader is Balidor. He is brilliant and daring, and his will is very strong. Even when he was a cub, there was no question that he would one day lead a pack. Before he led the Mystery, the pack meditated upon the earth spirit, offering it their strength and devotion. But when Balidor became leader, the Mystery began to seek ways to strengthen the earth spirit and weaken its enemies."

"I do not know how this can have anything to do with Ginger," Little Fur said. "Unless the wolves found out that he had just come from Underth. They might have thought he served the Troll King."

"Why would they think otherwise?" asked the wolf. "None use that road but trolls."

"Spies use it if they need to flee in a hurry and have become separated from their friends," Little Fur said.

"Then a spy would tell his tale," Graysong answered.

"The wolves might not believe it."

"Those of the Mystery can smell lies," said the old wolf. "Did the Sett Owl say anything more?"

Little Fur thought carefully before she spoke. "She said that I must find the Mystery of Wolves if I want to find Ginger. She also said that I must take the little owl who rides on my shoulder with me. But I do not see how a baby owl who cannot yet think clearly can help me in this."

"She will be a burden," Graysong agreed. "Let her fly back to the wilderness once we are in the open."

"She cannot fly," Little Fur said.

"Cannot," hooted Gem very softly.

Graysong looked at the little owl, no expression in his eyes. Then he padded ahead. They went on in silence along the tunnel.

Finally, Little Fur said, "The Sett Owl sent me to find the Mystery of Wolves. It was in seeking it that I found you, who can lead me there. Perhaps it is only when I reach the Mystery that I will truly understand the words of the Sett Owl."

"Perhaps," said Graysong, not even turning. "Perhaps not."

Although they were in the tunnel for some hours, no road serpent came along it. But when they emerged into the cold blue daylight, they heard the shriek of a road serpent. It took them a moment to realize that it was coming toward the tunnel.

The wolf bounded out of the channel over the snow that had tumbled down. Little Fur struggled to climb over the soft snow as the serpent roared closer. She would have joined the world's dream, but the wolf closed his teeth on her wrist and dragged her to safety as the road serpent

plunged into the mouth of the tunnel, throwing up a great spume of snow.

Little Fur lay against the soft, cold snow, heart

hammering, Gem hooting softly in her ear, until the thunderous shuddering of the earth subsided. Then she sat up and thanked the wolf gravely. He inclined his head equally gravely as she got to her feet.

They were now out of the city, and to Little Fur's surprise, they had also left the dense fog behind. She looked back where they had come from. There was the line of houses at the outer rim of the city. The towering high houses that rose up from its heart were still half wreathed in fog.

Little Fur looked ahead at a vast empty plain stretching to the horizon. White clouds massed up against the flat, gray sky. The blanketing snow hid the forests and hills, chasms and streams, birds and beasts in their nests and burrows and even solitary human dwellings. Little Fur had never been to the land beyond the city, yet she had heard of it from her friends. Her elf blood tingled at the idea of seeing it for herself.

By the side of a swift-running stream, she

stooped to take up a slender branch that would serve as a staff.

They had walked only a little way before she

realized that the distant clouds were mountains, marching high and jagged in both directions and out of sight. Her heart sank at the thought of Ginger crossing those mountains with Gazrak and the two ferrets. She found Graysong watching her, but as usual she could not read the expression in his eyes. Like his scent, it was very complex.

"Come," he said gruffly. "We must set a good pace and put the city behind us."

"Crow . . ."

"He will find us," the wolf said. He loped off, away from the shining tracks that ran across the land, toward the mountains.

"Crow," hooted Gem with longing.

Little Fur walked swiftly but steadily, following in the tracks of the wolf. Night came, and they walked into it. They had left all signs of humans behind. Finally, the wolf said that he needed to rest. Little Fur smelled his weariness and made no protest.

They found a good place to stop: a deep cleft

in the earth with several trees growing in it. The wolf ran down into the cleft and drank from a little winding stream as black as night between its white banks. Its current had kept it from icing over, but there was a thin crust of ice at the edges. Little Fur went down and drank in the coldness. She lifted the little owl down to drink as well, but Gem only shivered and closed her eyes. Sighing, Little Fur cuddled her close and looked up into the dark sky, wondering what had become of Crow.

The wolf sniffed out a tree that contained a hollow softened with a bed of pine needles. He curled into it, leaving room for Little Fur, but despite her tiredness, she wanted to explore. She asked Graysong if she could leave the owlet with him. He eyed Gem for a moment before nodding and laying his muzzle on his paws.

Little Fur lifted Gem onto his back, and the tiny bird settled into his thick, soft gray fur with a hoot of delight. Little Fur marveled that the tiny owl should have no fear of a wolf, to whom in other circumstances she would be prey.

Little Fur went to one of the trees and laid her hands on its knobbled bark. She found that the tree's sleep had deepened because of the cold, and she could not reach far enough to enter its dream. She did not try the other trees, knowing it would be the same, but she was pleased to find an unusual moss growing under one of them. It smelled as if it would be good for helping the edges of cuts grow back together. She took a small pinch, singing a song of thanks as she put it into her pouch.

A squirrel smelled Little Fur's activities and came out to chatter at her. Little Fur offered her a nut, and she hurried off to get a nut in return, as politeness among her kind required. When she came back, they exchanged nuts and Little Fur casually mentioned midwinter night.

"I would like to go to a Great Weaving some-day," said the squirrel. "But there are nuts to be found and nuts to be gathered and nuts to be stored."

"Of course," said Little Fur gently. "Have you seen any other creatures of the past ages traveling?"

"Not yet. Oh no. Not yet. But last year I saw a gargoyle going by. Very fearsome and noble, he

was. It was wonderfully terrifying, don't you know," the squirrel said doubtfully. Then she brightened. "But once, oh, this was wondrous! A tree sprite came! She stayed in my tree, and do you know it has given more nuts than any other tree ever since?" All at once the squirrel grew agitated and said she must return to her hoard.

After the squirrel had gone, Little Fur closed her eyes and tried to sense Ginger, but still she could get no feel of him. She thought of Crow and was delighted to sense that he was very close. She walked up out of the cleft and onto a mound of snow.

There he was—flying against the moon, which had just floated up into the sky. A few moments later, he landed beside her with a weary caw. Little Fur stroked his black feathers and fed him some seeds from her pouch, asking if he had gotten lost.

"Lost!" Crow gave an outraged croak. "Crow is never being lost. Crow is master of whereness of things." He went on to explain, with wounded dignity, that after she had gone into the tunnel with the wolf, he had flown back to the wilderness to let Tillet know what had happened at the beaked house. Little Fur was impressed, though she hoped for Tillet's sake that Crow had not exaggerated too much.

Little Fur asked if there was any news of the black dog. Crow grew so excited that he was unable to speak, and she waited until he preened himself calm. Then he told her that the black dog had never left the pony park. She had been there since the night they had found the sick human. Brownie's human had been leaving food out for her.

"Why?" Little Fur asked, amazed.

Crow fluffed out his chest, delighted to have her rapt attention. "No one knowing. But sameful every night. Human is putting out food and black dog is eating it, then running fastly away."

"But not to the wilderness!" Little Fur said.

"No," Crow said sulkily. He hated it when his audience guessed the ends of his tales correctly.

Little Fur showed Crow where the black
stream ran and waited while he drank. Then they
went back under the trees and got into the hollow
with Gem and the sleeping wolf. Crow slept
almost right away. Little Fur lay awake, listening
to the silence, broken occasionally by the sound
of snow falling. Gem woke once, and when she
saw Crow, her eyes glowed but she did not make
a sound.

Soon they all slept.

CHAPTER 7
The Crossroads

Little Fur woke to find that she was alone except for Gem.

"Stay here, you!" Gem said in a cranky Crow voice.

"Never mind," Little Fur said consolingly.

Gem began prodding a fluttering moth in a spiderweb, then ate it glumly. Little Fur picked the owlet up and climbed out of the hollow. The space under the trees was full of tattered violet shadows, but when she emerged from the cleft, the sun was shining a shy pink light on the snow. The wolf lay in the sun, licking his paws.

"I smelled humans, and I saw their tracks when I hunted at first light," the wolf said. "I have sent the crow to see if the way I want to go is clear."

Little Fur went back to the stream, washed her face and drank. This time Gem drank, too, and the wolf came to drink as well; then he stretched until his bones made a popping sound. They were standing beside the stream listening to its seductive tinkling music when Crow returned, screeching that the way was clear.

"Good," said Graysong, and they set off at once.

As they walked, Little Fur told the wolf what Crow had said about the black dog. Then she went back and told him about the sick human that had fallen into the wilderness. "I meant to ask the Sett Owl about the human, but I forgot."

"What would you have asked?"

"Why the trees allowed it to come," Little Fur said. But even as she spoke, she knew the answer. The trees prevented humans from entering the wilderness by turning away the minds of those who wanted to come there, but the sick human had not fixed its mind on it at all. Very likely it had not even seen the wilderness. Was there something in the encounter with the sick human that had made the black dog return to where she had dragged it?

Little Fur sighed. Being curious was very tiring. The Sett Owl had told her that curiosity was part of what made her a healer, and another time Sorrow had said that curiosity could be a kind of bravery.

"You smell of memories," Graysong said. "Are you thinking of your cat friend?"

"I was thinking of another friend—a fox who was born and brought up inside a human machine. Now he has gone to see if he can learn to be wild."

"Difficult," said the wolf.

"I think he might be the bravest creature I have ever known," Little Fur said fiercely.

They were following the course of a swift-flowing stream now. Little Fur thought they must be getting closer to the mountains, because they looked less like clouds and more like mountains. It was quite the loveliest thing to tramp along in the snow and never once pass anything you had seen before. In the wilderness, she knew every stone and hollow and every creature who dwelt there. Knowing it so well was part of what made it dear to her, but there was something wonderful in going where she had never been before.

At midday, they stopped to rest. Little Fur found a piece of cloth half buried under the snow. It was thick and beautifully soft, but it was too big to carry. She used her small stone knife to cut a piece large enough for a cloak, with a little extra for the pockets.

They continued on. Little Fur saw the tracks of many birds and of deer and foxes and rabbits. In the afternoon they came over a small rise, and there was a deer with her fawn eating the bark from a log of wood. They all froze, and Little Fur asked the wolf loudly if he meant to hunt. He said just as loudly that he had hunted already that morning and had no need of it.

Hearing these words, the deer relaxed, though she kept her eyes on the wolf as he walked to the top of a slope and lay down. Her fawn came forward on his spindly velvet legs as Little Fur approached his mother. Little Fur looked into his great dark eyes and saw her own face looking back at her.

"You are very new," Little Fur whispered to the fawn, staying very still and letting him sniff her. When he sniffed her hair, Gem's head popped out, and the owlet and fawn stared at one another in astonishment.

"Who?" the little owl hooted.

The fawn leaped into the air and came down in a tangle of legs that his mother had to sort out. Once her fawn had regained his legs, she nudged

him firmly aside and addressed Little Fur. "Why do you travel with a wolf?" she asked.

"He is leading me into the mountains," Little Fur said.

The deer's eyes went dark. "Then he leads you to your doom."

"He will not harm me," Little Fur said.

"Maybe he will and maybe he will not. But I do not speak of the wolf when I speak of danger. There is danger in the mountains."

"Hunters?" Little Fur asked.

"Not hunters! There is a deadly ice valley where all beasts who enter perish."

Little Fur was baffled. She asked, "Perish of what?"

But the deer was too frightened and upset to say anything more. She herded her fawn away. Little Fur returned to Graysong. As they set off again, she told him what the deer had said.

"It was just a story," Graysong said. "I know of no such place. Deer are full of fears and fancies."

Little Fur knew very well how tales could change shape when they were retold many times, but such tales always had a seed of truth in them. Yet she could smell that Graysong had made up his mind that the deer was mistaken. She was glad when they finally came upon a black road, so that she could fix her mind on something else.

There was no snow on the black road, which meant that road beasts had been along it recently, for the verges were thick with snow.

"We need not cross," Graysong said. "The road leads to a pass through the mountains. The Mystery is within the mountain peaks."

When the moon rose, casting its white, clear light, Graysong called a halt. Two road beasts had passed, and there was too much chance of their being seen if they continued. He had smelled a warm cave where a bear slept, and he led them there.

Normally bears were dangerously moody and

unpredictable, but this one was locked in an enchanted sleep that would not break until after the midwinter weaving. Emboldened by his stillness, Crow pecked lightly at the bear's shaggy coat, poked an inquisitive beak into his ear and finally flapped up onto the mound of the bear's belly to pace backward and forward, boasting that henceforth he must be called The Crow Who Stood on a Bear.

Perhaps his claws tickled the bear, for all of a sudden the beast gave a great snuffling grunt and rolled over, pinning the terrified Crow under an enormous paw. Crow gave a shriek of terror, and Gem, under the impression that her beloved brother was under attack, flew at the bear's face and pecked him on the nose.

Fortunately for all of them, Gem's tiny beak made no impression on the sleeping bear. Little Fur shooed her away so that she and Graysong could lever the bear's massive paw aside and release Crow.

By now Crow had swooned, and Little Fur dribbled water from her gourd into his beak to revive him. Crow pretended to remember none of it, but later she noticed him offer Gem a moth, saying carelessly that he had caught it without thinking and so she might as well have it.

They set off in the early hours of morning between

moonset and sunrise as a sleety rain fell and blurred the world. Crow flapped off with a dismal croak, but Gem gave a contented hoot and snuggled close to Little Fur's neck.

Little Fur was glad of the rain, for although no road beast had passed along the road yet, there were marks to show that several had gone by in the night, and more were likely to pass in the day. Rain, like night, would make it hard for the humans to see them.

By midday no road beast had gone by, and the rain stopped but the sky was a dull, dark gray that promised more snow before night. The pass had widened, and its steep walls now sloped backward. Graysong explained that they were entering a long sliver of a valley that ran lengthwise along the mountain range. The black road ran straight across the valley to another pass. There was also a place where a number of smaller roads set off in different directions. They would take one of these smaller roads up into the mountains.

"How long will it take us to find the Mystery?" Little Fur asked.

"Their territory is two wolf lopes away," the wolf answered. Little Fur smelled that this meant two days, for a wolf could lope for a whole day in his prime.

The sky had begun to darken again when Crow flapped down to say that there was a crossroads ahead. Suddenly they heard the low roar of a road beast. Looking back, they could see that it was moving very slowly. They had plenty of time to get behind some snowy shrubs. As it passed, Little Fur saw that it wore chains, and it clanked and crunched and groaned so laboriously along the icy road that she wondered if it was an old road beast.

"I need to hunt," Graysong said when the road beast was gone. "Keep going along the black road until you come to the crossroads. Find a safe place and wait for me."

Little Fur nodded. The wolf padded away, a gray shape only a little too light to be a shadow.

Two more road beasts passed before she reached the crossroads, but they did not slow. Little Fur found a clump of bushes growing over a big rock, under which there was a good dry den. It smelled of fox, but it was empty. The smell reminded her of Sorrow, and Little Fur hoped with all her heart that the gallant fox had found what he sought in the great wilderness. She lay down and slept, only to be awakened by a vixen. Little Fur was startled to see that she was entirely white.

"Greetings, vixen," she said politely. "I am sorry for the invasion. I thought the den abandoned."

"I abandoned it only two nights past, but something made me return," the vixen said. "Are you journeying to the midwinter weaving? Perhaps you do not know that there is no longer a ceremony in the mountains?"

"I am journeying to help a friend," Little Fur told her. "My name is Little Fur."

"My name is No-One," the vixen said.

"Little Fur!" Crow screamed.

Little Fur crawled out from under the bush to see the vulture from the zoo descending—but she was not attacking. She landed beside Little Fur and folded her feathers up.

"I have been looking for you, elf troll," she said.

"Why?" Little Fur asked, bemused.

No-One had come out now, too. Little Fur was fascinated to see that she was not white after all, but the palest glimmering silver gray.

"I have a message, so to speak," the vulture said. "Indeed, you might say I was given it because I was seeking you." She paused and looked at Little Fur, first out of one eye and then out of the other. She added, "The message was given to me en route."

"On the way?" Little Fur smelled the meaning of her words. "Who gave the message to you? A wolf?"

"I suppose you mean that wolf you helped to escape from the zoo. Oh, what a to-do there was! Who would have imagined such a fuss over a mere wolf? Of course, they have not even noticed *my* absence. So many humans running to and fro." She seemed disgusted, though whether it was because of the fuss over the wolf or the lack of fuss over herself Little Fur could not tell.

"Why did you go back to the zoo?" Little Fur asked.

"It was not my intention. I meant to fly away, but I kept ending up back there. It was most troubling. Then it came to me that perhaps I had not discharged my debt to you. I promised to get a key and I did not get it. So I decided to come see you and offer my service. I knew you were going to the mountains, and as soon as I thought of coming to you, I was able to leave the zoo. It is amazing what direction can come of a purpose!"

"You said there was a message?" Little Fur prompted the long-winded bird.

"Aha. Ah, yes. The message. Well. As I said, I was seeking you and I spied two nice ferrets. One of them was wounded, and I thought it would make a nice snack. But the she-ferret attacked me. Thin and weary she looked, but she attacked me so ferociously!"

"Two ferrets! What were their names?" Little Fur cried.

"Well, usually, you know, I do not ask the

names of my prey. It would be rude to eat someone whose name I knew. But I might as well have
asked, for in the end I did not eat her or her
brother. I told the she-ferret that it was her duty
to nourish one who had a debt to repay. She said
she had a vow to fulfill and that a vow was more
important than a debt. I asked what she had
vowed and to whom. 'I must deliver an urgent
message to the healer Little Fur,' she said. You
can imagine my astoundment. '*My* debt is to Little Fur!' I told her. Then I said that you had gone
to the mountains to save a cat. She gave a great
cry and said she must return to find you, but that
her brother was so ill, she didn't know how she
could. I offered to eat him and relieve her of her
burden, but she was most—"

"Did she say anything about Ginger? The
cat?" Little Fur interrupted.

"She said that he had been captured by—" She
broke off and frowned. "Was it a rat?"

"One of those he traveled with was a rat,"
Little Fur said.

"Really? A rat and a cat and two ferrets. How extraordinary. Well, I don't suppose it can have been a rat that captured the cat, in that case, though they are said to be dangerously clever creatures. . . ."

"Please! Try to remember who captured him?" Little Fur pleaded.

"Did she mention a human?" the vulture pondered.

"A human?"

"Perhaps it wasn't a human." The vulture sank her head into her feathers and gave a depressed sniff. "I knew there was too much to remember. Some of it must have fallen out as I was flying. But I do remember one thing. The she-ferret said that Little Fur must not . . . not . . ."

"Not . . . ?" Little Fur prompted.

"Risk yourself. He will free himself. That was the message. *Little Fur must not come to Ginger.*"

"I must go," Little Fur said.

"Oh dear!" said the vulture. "If only I could recall the rest." Her neck straightened out suddenly and rather alarmingly. "I must fly back and ask her! I'm sure she will not be too hard to find. The sick ferret was going very slowly. He might even have died," she added hopefully.

"All right," Little Fur said. "But I am still going up into the mountains."

"Very well," the vulture said. Her stomach rumbled loudly, and she glanced with wistful hunger at Gem. "I suppose you need that owl."

"Begone!" Crow screamed.

"I merely asked," the vulture said haughtily before flapping into the air.

"If the friend you seek is in the mountains, you must forget him," No-One said.

Little Fur looked at her. "Why do you say I should not go to the mountains?"

"Because beasts who go there die."

CHAPTER 8
The Fjord Spirit

The night had come, the silver fox had gone and a hazy moon had risen before Graysong returned. The old wolf insisted that they set off at once, for he meant them to reach the mountains by the morning.

When they reached another crossroads, Graysong said they would follow a narrow road of crushed rock. Little Fur scattered snow to let her cross the black road safely. The narrow road ran over flat ground at first; then it slanted and climbed the side of the valley. It narrowed further, becoming more of a track with a rock wall on one side and a sheer drop on the other.

"What if a road beast comes?" Little Fur panted.

"The way ahead was broken off by a rockslide when I was a cub," said Graysong. "What remains is too narrow for road beasts to pass."

Little Fur did not know whether to be reassured or to begin worrying about rockslides. To distract herself, she told the wolf about the news that the vulture had brought. Then she told him what the fox had said.

"You are still determined to go to the mountains?"

"Yes," Little Fur said. "The Sett Owl said I had to find the Mystery."

"She said you were to seek it if you wished to find your friend," Graysong said.

"Ginger would find me if I was in danger," Little Fur answered, a trollish stubbornness filling her.

Up and up they climbed as the moon marched

across the sky. Despite her worries, Little Fur's elf blood rejoiced in the sharp air and the bright moon. The night grew steadily colder, and finally Crow began to be troubled by it. When they stopped to nibble some of Little Fur's diminishing store of food, Little Fur wrapped the cloth and her arms about the black bird to warm him.

"Do we have to climb higher?" she asked Graysong.

"Another hour," the wolf answered. "Then we will need to find somewhere to rest properly."

The snow on the ground was very thick, and although Little Fur could make herself light enough to walk across the top of it, that was tiring, too. Whenever her concentration faltered, she would fall through the soft crust and have to dig herself out. It was three hours, not one, before they finally reached the summit.

Little Fur gasped. At the summit was a wide plateau encircled by snow-streaked black mountain peaks. A freezing wind blew into their faces, and caught helplessly in it, Crow was dashed against a stony outcrop. He fell to the snow and lay motionless. Little Fur gathered him into her arms again and wrapped the cloth around them.

"I need to get him to some shelter," she gasped.

"There is a cave, if you can carry him," Graysong said.

Little Fur nodded, hoping it was true. They headed for two peaks whose jagged tips leaned toward one another. The old wolf explained that the cave was in the first mountain, close to a narrow pass. Little Fur kept her eyes on it until the snow fell so thickly that she lost sight of everything but Graysong's shape ahead of her.

Little Fur was plodding along in a waking dream by the time they reached the twin peaks. She could not see them, but the wolf nosed along the rocks at the base of the mountain, smelling of certainty. She followed him, her arms burning from Crow's weight. The only parts of her that did not feel numb were where Crow was against her chest and Gem against her neck.

Graysong van- ished into a crack in the side of the mountain. Little Fur followed him. Inside was a vast dry cham- ber full of sinister echoes, but Little Fur's nose told her there was nothing dangerous. A collec- tion of snow bats

locked in their winter dream hung from the ceil- ing. Little Fur's troll blood surged with delight at being enclosed by the earth. She set Crow and Gem down, wrapping the cloth about them. Then she dug into the bottom of her pouch for a tiny set of flint stones given to her by a dwarf.

There was no wood, but Little Fur's troll blood told her there was black rock in the walls of the cavern. The dwarf who had given her the flint had said that black rock was what he used for the fires in which he smelted metals. She dug out a few chunks of the greasy black rock and heaped them about a pile of fibers she unraveled from one of the pieces of cloth she had intended to use as cloak pockets. She struck the flint and a spark fell at once, but she had to use her dried herbs as well as another piece of cloth to keep the flame alive long enough for the black rock to catch.

Little Fur had lit fires only a few times in her life. The sight of the leaping flames that she had summoned fascinated her so much that it took a moment for her to notice that Graysong was staring at her with a mixture of astonishment and wonder.

"It must be your elf blood that lets you do magic," the wolf said.

"I can't do magic any more than any other creature in this age," she laughed, and told him of the dwarf.

"But if your troll blood allows you to find this fire rock, why cannot your elf blood allow you to do magic?" the wolf asked curiously. "Were not

elves great magic workers in the last age?"

"No creature can do magic in this age."

"Is not the midwinter weaving a magic?"

Little Fur shook her head. "Only a ceremony

to break the unraveling winter dreams. We sing to weave them together so that the earth spirit can draw them into its flow. The weaving is a kind of guiding."

"Does not this Sett Owl use magic for her visions?"

"Better to say that the still magic that is in the beaked house uses her." She stopped, because she could see that the wolf's eyes were drooping in the warmth of the fire. Crow's eyes were closed, too, but Gem was staring into the flames.

Little Fur took the cloth, which the birds had shrugged off. Using a thorn needle, she began to sew the remaining scraps of cloth into a hood, since she had more need of that now than pockets.

The next day, when they left the chamber, it was not snowing. The sky was gray and hard like dirty ice, and a constant bitter wind blew, fanning the snow into cold flurries. Little Fur was glad that she had sewn a hood onto the cloth,

now nearly a cloak. They had been forced to leave Crow behind because he was still dizzy and his eyes were confused. Little Fur had wanted to wait until he recovered, but Crow insisted he would easily catch up to them once he was well enough to fly. In the meantime, Little Fur had left one of her precious seed pouches of food for him to eat and a pile of black rock broken into small pieces for him to add to the small fire that warmed the cavern.

Graysong said it would take one day of travel

to encounter wolf scouts who could lead them to the king. After two hours, Graysong turned into a narrow pass. It was angled so that as long as she kept to the one side, Little Fur was quite protected from the wind. They walked several more hours wrapped in silence before Graysong turned back to look at her.

"This pass will take us to the edge of a frozen fjord," he said. "We must cross it to reach the territory of the Mystery."

Little Fur suddenly wondered why the old wolf was helping her. He had made a bargain for his freedom, sure enough, but what could he do with it? Had he some thought of trying to join the Mystery? Certainly he could not long fend for himself alone.

It was over Graysong's shoulder that Little Fur first saw the long frozen fjord between the high walls of ice rising steeply up on both sides. "It is not more than an hour's walk to get across," Graysong said when they reached it.

Little Fur stepped out onto the ice. She shivered at the dense feeling of the magic that flowed through the water beneath it. She looked to where the fjord widened and ran out of sight between soaring ice banks. The wolf was staring

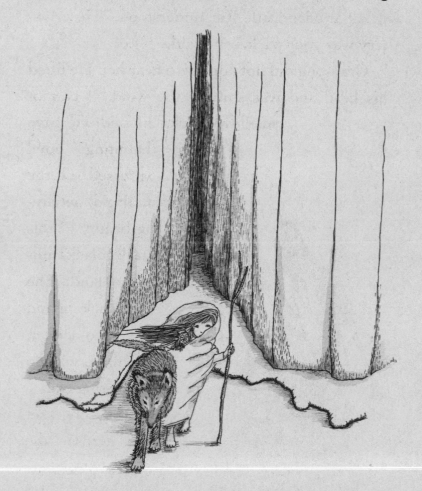

directly across the fjord, where there was a shore of snow. The old wolf trembled, and his scent was a mingling of tension and longing and apprehension.

All at once Little Fur understood. "The Mystery was your pack," she said.

Graysong did not appear to hear her. He lifted his head and was sniffing the wind. "I cannot smell the pack," he said. He gave a long, haunting howl that expressed all the vast, frigid, terrifying beauty of this stark black-and-white land. The cry was long and the echo longer, but there was no answering call.

Graysong set off across the

fjord, and Little Fur had no choice but to follow. The wind was behind them now, hurrying them along. When they were halfway across, it began to snow again, and the wind grew colder. For the first time in her life, Little Fur felt the cold as something cruel. But just when she felt she could not endure it any longer, the wind fell away, and all became utterly silent and still. It even stopped snowing.

Overhead, as if it had been waiting for this moment, a slit opened up in the clouds and a pallid radiance spilled down onto the ice. The white and gray became green and blue and violet.

"She comes," the wolf said, reverence in his voice. Then the smell changed. "She is angry."

"She?" Little Fur echoed.

"She," Gem hooted. Little Fur felt the frantic beat of the owlet's tiny heart.

Little Fur sensed an enormous surge of power beneath her feet. She looked down, and although the sun was not striking the ice where she stood, she could see a gorgeous rippling glow of deep violet blue. It was coming from under the ice. The ice began to crack.

"Run!" the wolf bayed, and bounded toward the snowy shore.

But Little Fur could not run. There was another sharp crack as the ice fractured in front of her. Then the ice broke open, and a great gush of water flowed up and out. Little Fur sensed that the ice under her feet had grown thin as an eggshell.

A head and shoulders emerged from the black water in the midst of the broken ice. Little Fur stared at the creature who stared at her. She looked like a water sprite but far more powerful. She was human-sized and had pale marble-white skin with long, furled ears and hair the color of ice that blushed at dawn, which flowed over her shoulders into the black water. Her eyes were a dark violet blue.

"You are of the last age," Little Fur said. "What is your name?"

"If you had one wish before you die, would it be to know my name?" the creature asked, her voice like the ice wind.

CHAPTER 9

The Elf Warrior and the Troll Princess

"You can kill me, for your power fills this fjord, Lady," Little Fur said to the powerful fjord being. "But I do not think you can grant wishes save if my wish is to know your name."

The creature's eyes became more violet. "You have trespassed upon a sacred place and must die."

"I am sorry that I trespassed," Little Fur said. "I did not know it was forbidden to walk here. A wolf led me here, but—"

"A wolf." The creature's white face pulled into a snarl, and her eyes went black as obsidian.

"Please," Little Fur said, struggling to keep her voice steady and strong. "He has not dwelt in these mountains for many seasons. He has been a captive of the humans."

"He led you here? Why?" the fjord spirit demanded.

"I seek the wolf pack that lives in this valley."

"There is no wolf pack here," she said. The darkness bled from her eyes, leaving them ice gray, cloud gray, wolf pelt gray.

"Please, Lady, do you know where they have gone?" Little Fur asked urgently. "I must find them, for I need their help."

"Wolves are faithless, and the one who led you here has brought you to your end."

"Do not harm her, Sjoerven," came Graysong's voice.

The old wolf had come back onto the ice. The fjord spirit looked at him. Little Fur saw a flash of violet joy in the gray of her eyes, then black rage. "If you care for her, Graysong, it will give me happiness to kill her."

"Do you hate me, then?"

"You left me!" A flare of anguish bleached the black from her eyes.

"I was driven out."

"Balidor was too young. But you let him win his challenge because he was your son. After you went, the pack left, too, though they had been here since the end of the last age."

"Why did they leave, Sjoerven? They would not have done so without the blessing of the fjord spirit."

"Balidor did not want my blessing," she said. "He asked a question and I visioned for him. Then he asked another question and I answered that. He left, then returned to ask a third question. When he left once again, he took the pack with him."

"What did he ask? What did you see?" Graysong asked.

"You know that none may know the question or vision of another," the fjord spirit answered.

"Then vision for me. Where is my son? Is he dead?"

"It would be better if he were," Sjoerven said. "But I cannot answer your question, for my mirror was taken."

"Taken! Who would dare?"

She looked at him. "Your son."

"Not possible," Graysong said, but suddenly he sounded old and weary.

"Your weakness allowed your son to steal from me, and so now I will steal from you." She turned again to Little Fur and flung out a slender hand.

There was a brittle cracking sound. Little Fur saw that the ice under her feet was so thin now that water seeped through it.

"I do not understand." The fjord spirit's face was haggard and beautiful and confounded. "The water will not obey me."

She glided closer, the ice melting away before her. Her eyes fell to Little Fur's chest, and to the green stone that hung there. "That!" she cried. "That protects her."

"It is not magic," Little Fur said, lifting it up.

"It belonged to one whom these waters were forbidden to harm," said the fjord spirit. She was so close now that Little Fur could see the sparkle of frost caught in her long indigo lashes.

"It belonged to my mother," whispered Little
Fur.

"Mother—" Sjoerven's eyes widened, and
storm blue became violet. "Then *you* are the one
she carried inside her! The child of the elf warrior and the troll princess."

Little Fur felt dizzy. "You knew my *parents*?"

"Yes," said Sjoerven. "I was a sprite in a
tiny streamlet that ran into a moat surrounding
a castle. There an elf warrior and a troll
princess were imprisoned by a powerful she-
wizard."

"Why?" Little Fur asked.

"They did not know, in the beginning. They knew little except mutual hatred, for each thought the other was in league with the she-wizard. But time passed, and eventually their long imprisonment and their alliance against the wizard caused the hatred between them to die. It must have died, for the troll princess soon carried the child of the elf warrior. Only then did the she-wizard tell them they had given her what she desired: a child in whom elf and troll blood mingled.

"The elf warrior swore that their enemy would not have their child," Sjoerven explained. "But before he could do anything, the land cracked open and the sea gushed inland, for the age of magic was ending. The ocean swallowed my stream and flooded over the castle, its power breaking the imprisonment spell at long last. But elf and troll remained trapped in a submerged chamber of the tower.

"The elf worked a mighty enchantment to hold back the sea. Then he cracked open the earth and bade the troll princess to escape, though he could not follow her into the earth. She left, for the sake of their unborn child. And the elf warrior was able to seal off her escape, but it took the last of his strength.

"The ocean flowed into the castle. I tried to save him, but the water was strong and I was yet weak. Eventually, I was able to bring him to the bank . . . too late, for he joined the world's dream. In his last moments, he gave me a mirror containing all that remained of his magic. And though magic was by then thin, I still grew to fill the fjord. Thus I became the fjord spirit. Now I am nothing, for the mirror is gone."

"I will find my son and return your mirror, Sjoerven," Graysong swore.

The fjord spirit looked at him, her eyes gone to silver. Without a word, she sank into the frigid black water. There was a crunching sound, and with a shudder, the ice thickened under Little Fur's feet and became solid—save for the jagged hole where the fjord spirit had first emerged.

* * *

They left the frozen fjord and climbed into a higher valley to rest and eat some pieces of honeycomb—all the food that Little Fur had left in her pouch.

"Did you let your son win the challenge?" Little Fur asked. It was easier to think about the wolves than to try to understand all that the fjord spirit had said of her parents and the she-wizard.

"I do not know," Graysong said. "Sjoerven was right in saying that Balidor was too young to lead. But he had such strength and such a fierce, pure desire to serve the earth spirit." He sighed.

"What do you think he asked the fjord spirit?"

"He would have asked how to fight the enemies of the earth spirit. He had long felt that I was holding the pack to a passive course. He wanted the Mystery to become an order of mystic warriors."

"That is why he challenged for leadership of the pack," Little Fur guessed. "But why would he take Sjoerven's mirror?"

"Not for the visions it would give," Graysong answered. "It would obey none but Sjoerven."

"But why did he leave? And where did he go?"

"I do not know, but you told me that the vulture that came to you while I hunted had said the cat had been captured by a human?"

"She said it might not be a human," Little Fur explained.

"It is only that returning to the mountains has reminded me of a story my grandsire told me of a human who built a keep in the mountains and filled it with its artifacts from the lost ages of the world," said Graysong.

"I don't understand," Little Fur said.

"The keep exists. I saw it when I was a pup. It was half ruined, and only a single old human dwelt there. It did not hunt or do any harm to beasts, but perhaps it has joined the world's dream and other humans now live there. Hunters."

"Why would they come to live in a ruin in the high mountains, and what does that have to do with the Mystery?" Little Fur said.

"The story my grandsire told was of a wolf who asked Sjoerven if there was any danger to the wolves in the keep. She is said to have answered that a terrible power would one day be born there, and that only a wolf would be able to prevent its destroying the earth spirit."

Little Fur was aghast. The Sett Owl had said nothing of this. "Do you think Sjoerven saw that

this power had been born? Maybe that is why your son went there?"

"I do not know, but I think we must go to the keep. It is far if we travel by smooth paths, but if you can climb, there is a swifter way."

"I can climb," Little Fur said stoutly.

The day grew colder and grayer as they ascended the steep flank of the mountain. Night came and the moon rose, blue and remote, as they climbed ever higher. The slope was now so steep that Little Fur did not dare to look down until they came to a ledge they could walk along. They drank some water, and only then did Little Fur look back over the flat whiteness of the frozen fjord far below. There was no sign of the strange spirit. They had followed the ledge path until it curved into another pass between two peaks. It sloped up, and they had to go on blindly, but at the top of the rise, Little Fur stopped to stare.

The path sloped down again, entering a small,

deep valley surrounded by high cliffs so steep
that no snow adhered to them. A human settle-
ment crawled up the cliffs, its many levels
connected by ledge paths or stone bridges or long
flights of steps cut into the cliffs.

CHAPTER 10
Wolf Keep

Whatever Little Fur had imagined when Graysong had spoken of a human keep in the mountains, it was not this!

"It did not seem so high or large when I was a cub," the wolf said.

"There is no false light," Little Fur said.

Before they could go more than a few steps, two wolves appeared from behind a snow-topped boulder just ahead.

"Scouts," Graysong murmured.

The wolves loped up to where he and Little

Fur stood. They were both large and strong, with ferocious eyes and lustrous fur, but a queer, almost-sick smell came from them.

"I am Sleet," said the she-wolf. She looked at Graysong. "I know who you are, Old Wolf. You should not have come back."

"I do not come to challenge or to rejoin the pack. I need to see my son," Graysong said courteously. "It is permitted by pack law."

"You will see him," said Sleet, a glimmer of malice in her gray eyes. "Come." She looked at Little Fur with an interest that made Little Fur's ears itch.

Graysong and Little Fur followed Sleet down the path. The silent he-wolf brought up the rear. Little Fur felt like a prisoner, and she was troubled by the wolves' smell. But most of all she was puzzled at the lack of surprise shown by the two wolves at coming upon their old king. Indeed, they had acted as if they were expecting him.

"You lead us to the human keep," Graysong said suddenly.

"Fear not, Old Wolf," answered Sleet, glancing back over her shoulder. "It is the wolf keep now."

"Why did the pack abandon its ancient territory on the banks of the fjord?" Graysong asked slowly.

Little Fur could see that Sleet did not intend to answer, but the other wolf's scent told her that he was having trouble refusing Graysong. He was older than Sleet, and Little Fur wondered if he remembered when Graysong had been king. At last, he said gruffly, "King Balidor said that we will better fulfill the true purpose of the Mystery here."

"Does King Balidor believe that the purpose of wolves can be found in the dwellings of humans, Nightwhisper?" Graysong asked.

Before Nightwhisper could reply, Sleet said coldly, "We have reclaimed this territory from the humans just as we will wrest the world and this age from them."

"An age is not a territory to be lost or claimed," Graysong said.

"I have heard it told that you were a king of subtle thought and many words, Old Wolf," Sleet said. "But now Balidor leads us, and he does not use words to strangle courage."

Nothing more was said for some time. They

were close enough to the wide gate in the wall to see a tumbledown sprawl of ruins in a cobbled yard. They seemed much older than the greater part of the keep. Where the cobbles showed through the snow, they were old and cracked. It was not until they passed into the yard that Little Fur saw that most of the keep had been cut out of and into the stone cliff. The ruined buildings, on the other hand, had been made of wood and stone and stood away from the cliff.

"The earth spirit is strong here," Graysong observed softly. "But it does not flow easily. Its currents flow in both directions."

Many of the wolves moving across the yard had stopped to stare at Graysong, but none came forward to greet him. Perhaps that was the way of the pack, but Little Fur's unease increased, for she could not smell surprise or shock on any of them. And clearly, the wolves were not captives here.

Graysong nudged her. Sleet had crossed the yard and was mounting a wide set of stone steps leading to an arch—the entrance to the keep. The she-wolf looked back impatiently.

Little Fur was relieved to find the steps, like most of the keep, were formed of living stone, through which earth magic could flow. What would Sleet have done if earth magic had not flowed through them and Little Fur had refused to follow her? She was trying to think how to explain her need to remain in contact with earth magic when a black she-wolf emerged from the shadows beyond the arch.

"Greetings, Graysong," she said courteously. "It is good to see you. I had heard that you were the captive of humans."

"Greetings, Shadow. I escaped from the humans with the help of my companion here. It is out of gratitude that I bring her to the Mystery. It took me longer to find it than I had expected."

Instead of answering his unspoken question, the black wolf looked at Little Fur, her yellow eyes glowing with interest. "Welcome, Little Fur.

The presence of a creature of the last age is welcome."

"Greetings, Shadow," Little Fur managed to say, astonished that the wolf knew her name.

"The king of the Mystery has bidden me welcome you to the wolf keep. I will show you to a place where you may refresh yourself and rest. Tonight there will be a feast. Have no fear of losing touch with the flow of earth magic, for most of the keep is made from living rock." She turned to Graysong. "Will you enter, Old Wolf?"

"I wish to see my son," Graysong said.

"Of course," Shadow said smoothly. "Nightwhisper will take you to a den where you can rest until the king is free to come to you."

Little Fur did not want to be separated from Graysong, but he appeared content for them to be parted, so she bade him farewell before he followed Nightwhisper away.

"Come," said Shadow. She went to a set of steps cut so cunningly sideways into the stone cliff that they were almost invisible. Little Fur followed warily until she had confirmed that there was no danger of her losing touch with the flow of earth magic.

The she-wolf had gone some way ahead before noticing that Little Fur had fallen behind. She waited until Little Fur caught up, then walked more slowly, speaking enthusiastically of the great feast being prepared. Little Fur asked its purpose.

"It is to welcome you, of course," Shadow answered.

Little Fur's mouth fell open in complete astonishment. "Me? But . . . why?"

Shadow did not answer. Perhaps she had not heard, for the loud roar of rushing water filled the air. In a moment, they had reached the top of the steps, which led to a stone bridge spanning a falling cataract of water. As they crossed, it became warm.

"Hot springwater is piped through most of the keep," Shadow said. "Humans like their dens hot."

"What happened to the human that used to live here?" Little Fur asked.

"It died," Shadow said indifferently.

On the other side of the bridge was another long stair leading up. This brought them to a ledge path that soon became a tunnel through the

cliff. Windows were open all along one side of the
tunnel, allowing air and light in. Little Fur gazed
out at the snowcapped mountains. She had never
been so high. This was how birds saw the
world!

Shadow stopped at the entrance to a small

chamber, inviting Little Fur to enter. She did so, startled by how warm it was.

As if in answer, Shadow pointed to a small bathing pool, from which steam rose. She bade Little Fur rest, promising to return when it was time for the feast. But Little Fur followed the she-wolf back out into the tunnel to ask how the wolves had known so much about her. The black wolf answered calmly that Balidor had told them.

Again she turned to leave, but Little Fur spoke. "Am I permitted to go out of this chamber?" she asked.

"I will take you anywhere you wish," the black wolf said smoothly. "But why not rest? King Balidor will show you everything this evening, and you smell of weariness and long traveling."

Little Fur nodded, still not sure if she was a guest or a prisoner. But it was true that she was weary. She thanked the black wolf and went back to the chamber, removed her cloak, pouch and water bottles and disentangled Gem from her hair. She set the little owlet on a bed of pine needles that had been prepared, and the owlet immediately began rearranging it. Little Fur took off the rest of her clothes and her necklet and climbed into the steaming water. It was surprisingly pleasant, and as she cleaned herself, her thoughts drifted to what Sjoerven had said about her mother and father. How queer to think they had both been captives of a she-wizard! And what had the wizard wanted with a child with elf and troll blood mingled?

Sjoerven had said her parents had begun by hating one another but had become allies. Yet they must have become more than allies to make her. At least for some moments, they must have loved one another. Was it love of the troll princess, then, that had made her father sacrifice himself to save her, or concern for the half-elf child she carried?

And what of her and her mother? The troll princess would have been able to use troll passages and tunnels to get to safety. Little Fur could almost imagine her flight, but where had she run? And what had happened to her, that Little Fur had ended up alone in the wilderness with a green stone and an elf cloak?

Not that she had truly been alone. She felt a pang of longing for the seven trees that had been mother and father to her. And then she thought of Ginger and realized with a shock that she had forgotten about him.

She got out of the water, dried herself and dressed hastily. Then she sat on a stone ledge, closed her eyes and brought Ginger's gray form to mind. *He was alive.* She would have known at once if he had perished. But the flow of earth magic was too disordered for her to feel him. She tried to reach Crow, but it was the same.

"Brother Crow," Gem hooted softly.

"Did you know what I was thinking, Gem?" Little Fur asked softly.

"Know," Gem hooted. She gazed through the window in the tunnel to where the moon was a small pale circle in a vast blackness.

CHAPTER 11
The King

"Wake, Little Fur. The king summons you," a voice said. "I am Cloud, come to take you to him."

Little Fur sat up, startled to find that she had fallen asleep when she had meant only to lie back and think. She had been dreaming of Ginger, but she could not remember what the dream had been about.

A light gray wolf stood by the door to the chamber. Little Fur got to her feet, leaving Gem behind, snuggled sound asleep in the pine needles.

"Where is Graysong?" Little Fur asked as she hurried to keep up with Cloud. The wolf was leading her along the tunnel to a set of ascending stairs.

"He sleeps," said the wolf.

"Isn't he coming to the feast?" Little Fur asked.

"The feast is not yet. The king wishes to speak with you before that. I am taking you to him."

The stairs brought them to a windy walk along the very top of the cliff. Cloud bade her go along it to where she would find the king. He was expecting her.

Little Fur saw no reason not to go. She leaned against the wind as she walked. Suddenly she saw an enormous wolf who had his front paws up on the low parapet and was gazing out at the mountains through which Little Fur had come. He was the most beautiful wolf Little Fur had ever seen. His fur was thick and white as new-fallen snow, and his eyes were the palest blue with a faint coil of cloud at their center.

"Greetings, Little Fur," the wolf said in a rich, deep voice. "Long have I looked forward to this meeting."

"Greetings, King Balidor," Little Fur said, bowing her head. "I am honored by your kindness, though I do not understand how you know me."

His eyes glowed with warmth. "Is there any creature in the land who has not heard the legend of Little Fur? She who fought the tree burners, who traveled to Underth and thwarted the devilish work of the Troll King? We are both warriors who strive to protect the earth spirit."

Little Fur blinked. "Graysong told me that the Mystery sought to strengthen the earth spirit."

"I see that Graysong has taught you the art of paring words. He was ever gifted at it. But surely one strengthens the earth spirit by protecting it, for then it need not squander its strength in defense. But come. I have much to show you, and a gift."

Thus Little Fur found herself walking the labyrinthine ways of the keep beside the glorious king of the wolves. Every wolf they passed bowed, but Balidor acknowledged none of them. His attention was all for her, and Little Fur was made shy by his intensity. She was bewildered by it, too. He had given her a reason for his warmth, but somehow it did not seem enough of a reason. Yet her nose told her that no lie had been told.

They passed through a chamber of musty-smelling objects that Balidor called books, which contained human runes. In them was all the knowledge of the humans. Little Fur looked about in wonder.

Balidor asked about her journey to the mountains. Little Fur told him of Ginger and her dream that he was in danger. The Wolf King smelled of polite attention until she mentioned the Sett Owl's advice to seek out the Mystery of Wolves. But the king was less interested in the Sett Owl's words than in the magic that produced her visions. He was especially interested in Little Fur's belief that humans created the still magic unwittingly when they came to the beaked house to sing and yearn. It cost her some effort to return to her story, so that she could describe her visit to the zoo and her meeting with Graysong.

"If Graysong has broken some law in returning here, I hope you will forgive it, since it was for my sake that he did so," she said earnestly.

"Do not trouble yourself about Graysong," said Balidor. "I have spoken to my father, and we understand each other very well." He went back to asking questions about the still magic. Finally, he said, "Imagine a vast pooling of magic in one beaked house, and no human knows it is there. Yet that magic might be used if one knew how."

Little Fur thought of Graysong's grandsire and his tale of a terrible power that would be born in the human keep, and that only a wolf could keep from destroying the earth spirit. Did Balidor imagine he was that wolf? Was that why he had taken Sjoerven's mirror? But if so, what was the power he must defeat?

Then, like the moon coming out from behind a cloud, her own purpose shone in her mind. "King Balidor, have you heard anything of the cat Ginger?" she asked.

"There is little in these mountains that escapes my eye, Little Fur," the white wolf answered. "Have no fear—you will soon be united with him."

Little Fur had hoped for a clear and simple answer. She wanted to press Balidor to say if he knew where Ginger was, but they were crossing another stone bridge now, and as they were high, it was windy. Balidor led her across it. Once they had entered a long chamber cut into the cliff, he spoke again.

"The one who made this keep was one of the few humans who understood about the other ages of the world. The tales humans tell one another are full of clues, and even as a youngling, this human heard the truth hidden inside the tales. Unlike most of his kind, he did not forget those truths when he grew to maturity. Instead, he set about trying to prove to other humans that the previous ages existed.

"After long years of study and travel, he found his first clue—a thing that belonged unmistakably to another age. After that, nothing could stop him. He became convinced that some few of the creatures of past ages dwelt in secret in this age. But though he found many rare and strange artifacts, his greatest aim was to find a creature that could work magic. His deepest desire was to restore magic to the world. He did not understand that all of the creatures who could work magic had perished."

The wolf stopped before an archway. The door that had once fitted into it hung sagging off its hinges. Through it was a very long, narrow chamber with small windows cut high into the stone along the side of the chamber. Many panels of unmelting ice were fixed to the walls beneath the windows. Objects hung behind the panels and sat on shelves or tables.

"This is the treasure room of the human! All of the things he collected are here," said the Wolf King. "Pixie daggers, dwarf hammers, the medicine horn of a centaur, the comb of a mer-maiden, pearl hair clips of sea sprites. The human arranged his treasures like this so that he could show other humans and share his dream. But of those who came, most went away to tell tales of a great mountain folly built by a madman. A few stayed for a time, but in the end, the human who built this was alone."

Balidor moved closer to the cases as he spoke,

and suddenly Little Fur saw something, behind one of the panels of unmelting ice, that took her breath away. It was her father's gray cloak!

"Your eyes are sharp, Little Fur," approved Balidor. He stepped forward and lifted a paw to press a metal form set into the unmelting ice. The front part sprang open like a door. The Wolf King nosed it open properly and said, "Take what is your own."

Little Fur reached up, feeling as if she had stepped into a dream. Her fingers closed about the soft folds of the gray cloak, and she took it down and pressed her face to it. Before it had been stolen from her, she had valued the cloak for its powers. But now she sniffed it, hungry to find some scent of her father. Suddenly he was not an unknown elf. He was an elf who had been imprisoned by a wizard—an elf who had held back the sea and cracked open the earth. He must have given this cloak to her mother. How else should it have come to belong to Little Fur with the green stone?

"Finally, another human brought him a few pages from a wizard's rune book," the wolf continued. "The runes showed him that magic could be taken from a creature of the past ages of the world and put into a human. With it, that human would be able to work magic, because this was the age of humans."

Little Fur felt bewildered by the things that the wolf was saying. There seemed to be madness in his words, and the almost-sickness that she could smell on all of the wolves was suddenly very strong.

"I thank you for this cloak," she managed to say. "But, King Balidor, how did you know it was mine? Did the mirror of the fjord spirit tell you?"

For a moment, all color seemed to fade from the wolf's eyes, leaving them white and blind-looking. But he did not smell of surprise. "Gray-song said that Sjoerven threatened you but could not harm you. I am glad of it. She also told you that I stole her mirror. It is not true. Sjoerven offered it to me, and she commanded it to show me all that I asked to see in it. I do not know why, for there is no love between us. No doubt she has come to regret giving it away, and that is why she lied."

Now there was anger in his eyes, but it only made him look more handsome. "Sjoerven weakened my father and the pack, so I was forced to challenge him, though I was not truly old or wise enough to become king, and he was not ready to be unmade."

"He does not seem weak to me," Little Fur said.

"He is not," Balidor said. "The fjord spirit used his wisdom against him. She prevented him from seeing what he might have seen without her."

"What is that?" Little Fur asked softly.

"That humans are the greatest danger to the earth spirit and to all of the things that remain from the last ages of the world. Without them, your kind would not have to hide or keep themselves secret. If humans did not exist, earth magic would flow through everything. Humans are the true enemy of the earth spirit."

"But you have said yourself that this is the age of humans," Little Fur said. She was about to add that her adventures had also taught her that not all humans were black-hearted monsters bent on destruction, but Balidor spoke first.

"It is their age," he said. "But do you not work against them every time you plant a seed in their city to strengthen the flow of earth magic?"

Little Fur was taken aback. "I am merely trying to make the flow strong enough so that humans will feel it. Then they will understand—"

"Understand what?" Balidor demanded. "That they are not the masters of the world, but only a part of it, just as the smallest saplings or wolf pups are?"

"But once they know what it is to be a part of—"

"Little Fur." Balidor cut off her words gently. "Your heart is great, and I honor you for it. But humans do not see that they are part of the world. They know what they do harms other creatures and even their own kind, but they do it anyway. That is why trolls thrive in this time, and plot endlessly against the earth spirit. Wipe the race of humans from this age, and you will end the race of trolls as well."

"Wipe—what do you mean?"

The wolf blinked. "I meant only that we must fight humans and all their works. But come, let me show you what else is here." He led her around more of the unmelting ice panels. Little Fur was dizzied to see the wings of a fairie, the horn of a unicorn and the carvings of tree pixies, and even runes like those she had seen on the way to the troll city of Underth. A great sadness crept into her, for all that Balidor had said was true.

Shadow padded into the long chamber and spoke quietly to the king.

Balidor sighed and turned his pale, lovely eyes on Little Fur. "I wish I might spend long hours

here with you, but I must be king. Cloud waits outside. He will escort you back to your chamber when you are ready. We will see one another tonight."

Little Fur did not tarry long after the king had left, for she was worried about Gem. As she walked along with Cloud, she thought about the Wolf King. Balidor had been more beautiful and compelling than she had expected. But her meeting with him had raised more questions in her mind than it had answered.

Thanking the old wolf, Little Fur went back inside the chamber and nearly fell over in surprise. There stood the red-eyed rat Gazrak, whom she had last seen escaping from Underth. And with him was Crow!

CHAPTER 12
The Joining

"Gazrak! What are you doing here? Where is Ginger?"

"Gazrak will answer if Little Fur stops asking so many questions!" the rat snapped. He cast a warning look at the open door to her chamber. "Be quietful or the wolves will come."

Little Fur could smell the rat's fear. A wave of apprehension rose up in her. "Tell me everything," she urged softly.

"No time for so much telling," the rat said. "Gazrak will begin at the ending. We came to the mountains and Ginger was caught in a trap. Wolves came and freed him. He was bleeding and they brought us here. They promised to heal Ginger."

"Ginger is here?"

"You are very interruptful," Gazrak snapped. "Ginger is here! Is not Gazrak saying it already! All of us are here, and then the king of wolves says Ginger must stay until his paw is healed but we threesome must go home. Shikra said we will wait, but the Wolf King forbade it. Shikra asked if she could speak with Ginger, but the Wolf King said he was sleeping and that we must go to Little Fur and invite her to visit wolf keep. Gazrak smelled sharp teeth and dangerousness behind his inviting. We went, but when the wolves stopped following, we hid in a cave. Then Gazrak crept back and sniffed out the cat. He was in a cave with bars, and there was a chain on his leg. He said that he would free himself when his paw was healed and we must go as the Wolf King commanded. But we must tell Little Fur *not* to come to the mountains."

Little Fur's thoughts whirled like snowflakes in a storm. "Gazrak, where is Ginger? Take me to him."

"No!" Gazrak cried, gnashing his teeth. "Little Fur not listening—you must leave! Why you are here? Did not Shikra instructioning you not to come?"

"I didn't see Shikra. I came because the Sett Owl—"

"Sett Owl," Gazrak sighed. "Happiest days of Gazrak's life were with Herness. All else has been dangerful darkness."

"Gazrak, the Sett Owl told me to find Ginger. You must take me to him. I won't give up."

"I told you so," crowed Crow to Gazrak. Little Fur gave him a quick hug. Then she put wide-eyed Gem on her shoulder, donned her green stone and bade Crow fly outside to await them.

"We'll all be killed," moaned Gazrak.

"Don't be afraid," Little Fur told him. "I have a cloak that will hide us from the wolves. We will all escape together just as we escaped from the trolls in Underth."

"And look where that getting us," Gazrak muttered. He sniffed and sighed, and then he nodded. "All right, but if Ginger bites Gazrak, Gazrak will be biting Little Fur very hardly!"

Wrapped in her father's cloak, with Gem upon her shoulder, Little Fur padded softly after the rat. There were many wolves about, but Little Fur kept to the shadows, and the cloak helped keep her scent close. Once Gazrak had to cause a slight distraction to allow her to get through a room where wolves were clustered, dividing up a boar they had killed. Little Fur understood from

their words that the dead beast was being prepared for something called the Great Joining.
The word reeked of almost-sickness.

Once they were past the group of wolves, they
went deeper in the labyrinth of chambers and
paths. There were a good many fewer wolves in
the lower levels of the keep. Little Fur wondered
how much of Balidor's tale about the human was
true. The treasures it had collected showed that
the human had proven the existence of creatures

from another age. It must have bought or stolen her cloak from the human that had taken it, but that still did not explain how Balidor had known it was hers. Nor how he had known so much of the human's story. The only answer could be the mirror.

When they came to a ramp leading down to a door, Gazrak spoke: "Here is the chamber where are the prisoners of the Mystery kept."

"We will need a distraction to get the guards out," Little Fur said.

"No guardians are here," Gazrak said. "Ginger is behind strong bars. He is not needful of guarding."

"All right," Little Fur said. "You wait here in that crack in the wall." Little Fur removed her seed pouches and water gourd, putting them along with Gem in the crack so that she would be unhampered if she had to run. "Protect her," she told Gazrak.

"Protector," Gem said, regarding the rat solemnly.

The rat's mouth fell open.

Little Fur hurried down the tunnel and entered a wide, low-roofed chamber with an earthen floor and stone walls. Her troll senses told her that she was below the level of the ground now. It was the work of a moment to find Ginger, but her heart sank at the sight of the thick bars and the heavy lock. Hiding her despair, she reached out through the bars to lay her hand on Ginger's back.

He sat up slowly, and Little Fur smelled at once that he had been given a potion to make him sleepy. But he fought the fog in his mind and turned to look at her. There was love in his brilliant eyes.

"I dreamed that you would come," he sighed in his deep, velvety voice. "I wished it and feared it."

Little Fur slid her arms between the bars and put them around the big gray cat, pressing her face into his dense fur and drawing in the dear, warm smell of him. He felt thin under the thick

fur, but he purred, and they sat like that for a long moment.

Finally, Little Fur pulled herself away. "Ginger, I know you tried to stop me from coming here, but the Sett Owl told me that I must come—"

"I knew you would go to her," Ginger said. "I thought she would warn you that it is a trap."

"A trap?!"

"It is you that the Wolf King wants. I am only the bait," Ginger said.

Little Fur stared at him. "I . . . I don't understand. Why does the Wolf King want me?"

"I do not know what he wants of you," Ginger said. "He has a magic mirror, and it showed him something about you."

"The mirror told Balidor that you have the power to change the world. It is the power of your elf blood that Balidor lusts after," said another voice. It was a familiar one, and somehow it did not surprise Little Fur to hear it here. After a soft, swift explanation to Ginger, she

went along the little cavern cells until she found
the one where Graysong lay. He smelled of pain,
and Little Fur saw the bloody bite mark on his
back leg.

"What happened?" she asked, reaching for her
healing pouch before remembering that she had
left it behind.

"My son . . . attacked me," the old wolf said.
"Sjoerven was right. Love made me weak. All of
this is my doing."

"Hush," Little Fur said. "I will go and get my healing pouch."

"Do not waste your healing on me," Graysong rasped. "Leave this place at once, for your friend is right. It is you whom my son wants."

"There is no power in my elf blood, save that it lets me love the sky and the sun and all green and growing things," Little Fur said.

The old wolf heaved a great sigh. "The human that made this place learned of a substance which can hold a spirit that has departed from its body. Unable to fly away, the trapped spirit will enter the body of anything that lives. The human created a chamber and experimented with beasts, killing one and seeing its spirit enter the other."

"But what has this to do with me, or Balidor?" asked Little Fur. "The human is dead."

"It was not dead when I left the pack. Nor was it dead when Sjoerven told my son that a dark power would be born in the human keep. Balidor came here to learn what that power might be, and he was captured by the human. It had decided to take into itself the spirit of a beast, in the hope that this would better enable it to find a creature of the last age. But something went wrong, and instead of my son dying, the human perished and its spirit entered my son."

"What?" Little Fur whispered, horrified.

"My son bears the spirit of a human, and the human's desires have merged with Balidor's. The human sought to gain the magic of the last age, and now that is what Balidor wishes. He returned to the fjord and asked Sjoerven if there was any creature alive in this age able to work magic. She offered him the mirror and bade it show him what he wished to see.

"I do not know what he asked, but the mirror showed him your face, and it was the mirror that told him your cat friend was coming through the mountain pass. A trap was set, and once Balidor had the cat, he knew he had only to wait for you to come."

"He means to eat my spirit?" Little Fur asked.

She was remembering the eagerness she had smelled on the Wolf King.

"He does. He believes that once he has your spirit, he will be able to work magic. That is how he would protect the earth spirit."

"What will happen to me?"

"Your body will die. Your spirit will live until Balidor dies."

"He told you all of this?" Little Fur asked.

"Balidor said that he wanted me to understand. I told him that if he consumed your spirit, the earth spirit would recoil from him in horror. That is when he attacked me."

"I will free you both," Little Fur began. "I will find the keys."

"It is too late," said the old wolf, his eyes full of pity. "Balidor knew that you would come here. He saw it in the mirror. He is watching us now. There is no escape."

He looked up, and Little Fur did the same. Balidor, Shadow and several other wolves gazed down at them from a stone ledge.

CHAPTER 13
Spirit Eater

They stood on the wide, flat plateau of stone at the topmost level of the keep. Behind them, the black cliff rose sheer and high, and around them lay the dark, snowy peaks of the mountains. The moon had set and the sun had yet to rise, but a faint glow of false light came from a gleaming bubble of unmelting ice. Nightwhisper had told Little Fur this was the spirit chamber and the glow was the substance that would stop a spirit from escaping, but it needed light, and so they were awaiting sunrise.

"You should feel honored," Balidor said to Little Fur. "You will help to restore magic to the world, and there can be no greater healing."

"There is magic already in the world," Little Fur said. "Earth magic churns under my feet."

"It churns in excitement," said the white wolf. "For tonight, the earth spirit will see the birth of one who will be able to work magic, as wizard- and elf-kind did in the last age."

"And what will be the first act of this creature?" Graysong demanded from where he lay. "Death and destruction."

"Death to the dealers of death. Destruction to the humans that do nothing but destroy," retorted Balidor. "Now be silent, Old Wolf, lest I regret my indulgence in allowing you one last chance to witness the greatness of your son."

"This is the age of humans," Little Fur said. "None can work magic in this age, least of all me."

"Tonight our spirits will be joined," Balidor said. "And in six nights, when midwinter comes,

I will swallow the dreams of winter. And then I will go to this beaked house and use its magic to wipe humans from the earth."

The reek of almost-sickness flowing from the Wolf King was overpowering. Despite her terror, Little Fur felt a surge of pity for him. "This mingling of spirits has made you ill," she said. "Let

me try to heal you. It is not your fault that the human's spirit entered you. Perhaps it can be released."

Balidor gave a growling laugh. "The human thought I was near death when it closed itself in the spirit chamber with me. But I sprang at it and tore its life out, and then I ate its spirit. As I will now eat yours."

Little Fur turned to look at Shadow, who stood by Balidor's side. "How can you let this happen? Can't you smell the wrongness of it? What happened with the human was its own fault, but if Balidor does this, it will be of his own choosing."

"Balidor is king," Shadow said in her hard, clear voice. "A wolf of the pack obeys her king without question in all things. That is the law."

"Balidor is no longer a true wolf," Little Fur said. "He is part human, and he cannot be your king."

"Silence!" Balidor said. "Put her into the spirit chamber."

"The king breaks the law of the pack if he does this." Graysong's voice rang out.

A shocked smell flowed from the assembled pack.

Balidor stalked over to his sire. "I brought you to witness a great thing, Old Wolf, and you tell me that I break the law of the pack? There is no pack law that forbids killing. Nor the killing of an outcast wolf."

"I must be heard. That is the law of the pack."

"It is true, King," said Nightwhisper, who had been standing guard over the old wolf.

"I know the law," snarled Balidor. "Let him speak his charge before I kill him."

Nightwhisper nosed Graysong to his paws. The old wolf looked beaten, but his eyes glowed with blue fire when he looked at his son, and then at the other wolves. Slowly he straightened and lifted his head. Little Fur had a glimpse of how he had looked in his prime when he was king of the pack.

"Speak," Balidor commanded.

"The wolf pack keeps its oaths, King, is it not true?"

Balidor looked puzzled. "It is true. The youngest cub knows it. Do you think I have forgotten it? Or any of those assembled here?"

"Then you cannot harm Little Fur, for a blood oath protects her."

"You are not part of the Mystery. If you swore to protect her, you made your oath as a lone wolf."

"It was not I who swore it but a wolf who was king."

"You claim to have made an oath when you were king?"

"Not I, but the *first* king—he who was born in the last days of the last age. You know of whom I speak?"

"Brightmane, first of the wolves," Balidor said. "But what oath could he have made that affects Little Fur?"

"Elf blood runs in her veins," Graysong answered.

"I know it. But Brightmane made no oath to spare the blood of elves."

"No, yet he swore a brother oath to one elf—to Ardent, by whose side he fought a war. Little Fur is the daughter of Ardent."

"Impossible. Little Fur is half troll! Never would Ardent have consorted with a troll."

"Ardent died for the troll princess as Brightmane died for him. And a brother oath is a blood oath. You cannot shed Little Fur's blood, or you

194

break the oath of Brightmane to Ardent."

"How do you know this? Maybe it is a lie," Balidor growled. His words caused a stir of unease among the wolves.

"A wolf does not lie," Graysong said gravely.

"I meant that you may have been told a lie," Balidor said, bluster in his voice. "Where did you come by this story?"

"The fjord spirit told it to Little Fur. And it was not a story but a thing Sjoerven witnessed in the last age when she was but the sprite of a small stream. As you know, her mirror was bestowed upon her by Ardent, who died on the shore of the fjord in her arms. The choosing of the fjord valley as our territory was the pack's way of remembering

Brightmane. Little Fur's blood is the reason Sjoerven could not make the waters of the fjord harm her."

"The mirror did not show any of this to me," Balidor growled.

"That is because Sjoerven bade the mirror show you what you *wanted* to see. It could not show a lie, but it did not show you any truth that you would not want to see. And now I say again to you, you must not shed the blood of Little Fur."

There was a resounding silence. Little Fur could smell the confusion of the wolves and see it in the looks they exchanged and the way their fur crackled with indecision.

Balidor turned to them. "What I will do this night will break no oath, for the spirit of Little Fur will not perish. It will live on in me, the king, and is it not fitting that the King of the Wolves should join with the daughter of Ardent, who swore blood oath with Brightmane? There is a greatness that stirs my blood and tells me that what we do this night is a noble deed. Did not Little Fur come here of her own accord? She has spent her life healing and serving the earth spirit, as has the Mystery. It is fitting that we join spirits now and turn our wills to free the earth of humans."

There was a glorious certainty to Balidor's words, and Little Fur could feel the doubts of the pack fading. Added to Balidor's beauty, their every instinct and desire was to obey their king.

"You argue like a human," Graysong said.

"Silence," Balidor said coldly. "You have made your charge, Old Wolf, and I have answered it."

"My king, I have a doubt," said a new voice. It was Nightwhisper, his head hung low to show respect.

"Speak," Balidor said.

"Perhaps it would be better to go and speak with Sjoerven before this thing is done. To see if this joining will truly serve the earth spirit."

"Are you challenging me?" Balidor asked in a low, fierce voice.

"No, my king. I only—"

"Then obey me!"

Balidor turned to the rest of the wolves. "Do any of you wish to challenge me? If so, do it now."

None of the wolves spoke. Several had dropped to their bellies in a display of obedience. Balidor

turned to Nightwhisper and said, "The sun is near to rising. Put the healer into the spirit chamber."

Graysong spoke quickly. "My son, did you never wonder why Sjoerven gave her mirror to you?"

Balidor glared. "What do you mean?"

"Did it never occur to you that she sought to revenge herself upon you — for driving *me* away — by ensuring that the mirror would tell you only what you wished to know rather than what you needed to know?"

"What do I need to know?" Balidor's voice lashed out.

Graysong sank to the ground, his legs too weak to hold him. There was blood all along his side. "I . . . cannot tell you," Graysong rasped. "I break no law in refusing to speak, for I am no longer of this pack, and you are not my king."

"Then I will eat your spirit and learn what I need to know that way!" Balidor snarled. He lunged at his father and closed his teeth in the old

wolf's mane. Gray-
song did not
struggle as Bali-
dor dragged him
into the spirit
chamber.

"Close it!" Bali-
dor snarled.

"We must do
something!" Little
Fur whispered to Ginger, who lay with his paws
bound beside her.

"Being quietful is what you can do," hissed a
voice.

Little Fur looked down in astonishment to see
Gazrak half hidden under Ginger's tail. His red
eyes shifted from her to the spirit chamber, and
his nose trembled with purpose. Little Fur had
not seen the rat, Gem or Crow since the wolves
had taken her captive. Gazrak must have sniffed
his way to the roof of the keep after them. But
what was he trying to do?

Suddenly a loud humming sound filled the air, and a great transparent bubble closed over the metal plate on which Balidor stood above Graysong's prone body. Beyond it the mists that filled

the deep little valley and wreathed the mountain
peaks were flushed with delicate pink and a faint
gold. A rainbow rippled over the spirit chamber
as the first rays of sunlight streamed out, and
Balidor looked down at his father.

"Tell me what I need to know now and I will spare you, for you were once king of the wolves, and you were once my father," Balidor said.

"I am *still* your father," Graysong said, and he leaped and sank his teeth into his son's throat.

Balidor gave a howl and reared back in shock and pain. Then he lashed out with his forepaws and shook his head. He was powerful and young, but Graysong was grim and tough, and he did not let go. There was a long, nearly silent struggle, hard to see in the shifting rainbow and in the mist of the wolves' breath that filmed the inside of the unmelting ice. Then came a deadly quietness, broken by a long, desolate howl that sounded of deepest grief.

"Open it!" snarled Shadow, hurling herself at the chamber.

Slowly the bubble rose with a hum, throwing out knives of brightness. Graysong was standing over the body of his son. Gazrak scuttled through the pack of shocked wolves, but Sleet slapped her paw down on his tail, bringing the rat to a

halt so sharply that he squealed with pain. Crow swooped out of nowhere to attack Sleet with such a furious cawing force that the wolf flinched, releasing Gazrak. The rat was up in a second and across to the spirit chamber, where Graysong still stood. The old wolf lowered his anguished gaze to listen to the rat, then he opened his jaws and let Gazrak put something into his mouth.

"King Graysong," Nightwhisper said, suddenly and loudly. "You have challenged and won. Command us."

Graysong looked at him, and the anguish of a moment before was gone. "Yes, I am king. It is my first and last command that you go from this place and live as true wolves. Obey the law of the pack. Keep your oaths."

Then Graysong fell dead over his son's body.

CHAPTER 14

The Great Weaving

"I do not understand," Little Fur said.

"I think I do," Ginger said softly. It was snowing lightly, and the flakes lay in a soft white dappling over his fur. "Graysong goaded his son into the chamber so that he could take his spirit. It was the only way he could prevent Balidor from breaking a blood oath. The only way to prevent him from becoming a monster."

"And Gazrak?"

"He took the nut with the poison from your

healing pouch, and he gave it to Graysong because Gem bade him do it."

"She must have seen that he would not want to live, having killed his own son," Little Fur said.

"That," Ginger agreed, "but also I think Gem foresaw that the madness which corrupted Balidor could do the same to Graysong. She was making sure that did not happen." Ginger paused for a moment. "She is a seer, of course, just as the Sett Owl is."

Little Fur shook her head. "I always thought the Sett Owl's visions came from the still magic."

"So did I, but it must be that the still magic chose the Sett Owl because of what she was. And now Gem will go to the beaked house, too."

"I think the Sett Owl was trying to tell me about Gem, but I was too anxious about you to listen," Little Fur murmured. She looked to where the owlet sat on a boulder between Crow and Gazrak, who had already declared himself protector of the small Herness. "I wonder what she told Gazrak to say to Graysong."

"I asked, but he refused to tell me. He said it was between him and the small Herness. I don't suppose Gem will tell me either."

Little Fur nodded somberly.

Ginger continued, "But for my part, I am most curious about what the Sett Owl will say when she realizes that she is going to have to put up with Crow's singing to gain an apprentice." He sounded amused.

"Perhaps she knows," Little Fur said, and she hugged the gray cat, her heart suddenly brimming with the joyous knowledge that she had succeeded in her quest to find him.

Nightwhisper approached. "We are ready. The spirit chamber has been destroyed." He looked back at the towering human complex that cleaved to the black cliffs. "Balidor was a noble wolf. It was the human spirit that twisted his mind."

"His spirit is with his father's now," Ginger said.

The gray wolf looked at the gray cat. "I am sorry we trapped you and kept you prisoner, Cat."

"It is finished," Ginger said.

They could not use the steep, swift trail Little Fur had taken with Graysong because of the litter bearing the bodies of the two dead wolves. Crow flew part of the way with them, before flying ahead to let Tillet and the ferrets know they were safe and on their way home. But it was too late for Little Fur and the others to get back to the wilderness in time for the weaving, so Little Fur meant to hold her own small ceremony at the fjord.

As they traveled, it snowed lightly but constantly, though the wind seemed to have spent all of its vicious force. Little Fur hardly noticed, since her mind was full of memories of her journey with Graysong. So much had happened since she'd freed him from the zoo that she had hardly noticed how much she had come to admire the tough old wolf. It saddened her that she would never see him again.

Yet she was consoled by her certainty that Graysong's spirit was serene. Had he not saved the earth spirit from the danger that had been born in the keep, just as Sjoerven had foretold? Had he not saved his son from what he might have become? She had only to see how tenderly his muzzle rested beside his son's to know that both wolves were at peace.

She thought about her own father, whose name the wolves had spoken, unaware that she

had not heard it before. Ardent. Ardent, who had held back the sea and opened the earth for an unborn Little Fur and her mother. Ardent, to whom a wolf king had sworn a blood oath.

On the last day of the journey to the fjord, Little Fur found herself thinking again of the final moments of the wolves' lives. She said to Ginger, "Graysong said there was something he knew, something that Balidor needed to know. I wonder what it was, for he never lied."

"I think it was only that Balidor was wrong about saving the earth spirit by killing humans,"

Ginger answered. "Or maybe that he was wrong about being able to work magic if he stole your spirit."

By the time they arrived at the fjord, the moon had risen and was shedding a silvery radiance that made the snow glisten.

"What are you thinking about?" Ginger asked.

"I was thinking that somewhere under the ice is the place where a wizard imprisoned my mother and father, and I don't really know why."

"You could ask the fjord spirit to look in her mirror," said Gazrak, who had come to sniff suspiciously at the ice.

"I could," said Little Fur.

Little Fur went ahead with Ginger and Gazrak as new wolves took over pulling the pallet bearing their kings down to the level of the ice. Gem was on her shoulder and under her hair, but her beak popped out occasionally.

"How do you get her icefulness to come out?" asked Gazrak, sniffing curiously at the ice.

"You must walk on the ice," Nightwhisper said, coming to stand with them. He gave a sigh, rather like someone about to take up a burden he knows will be heavy and tiresome. Then he walked onto the ice, lifted his head and howled.

At first, there was a loud *crack,* and then a cavalcade of smaller *snap*s. The ice broke open and Sjoerven rose.

"What do you want of me, Wolf?" she asked. Her eyes went from Nightwhisper to the rest of the pack along the bank and to Little Fur and her companions.

Then she saw the pallet upon which the two dead wolves lay.

"Graysong." Her voice was a shriek of wind over a desolate plain in the darkest hour of night. Her violet gaze shifted to Balidor. "Both of them? But how?"

In answer, Little Fur came and held out the 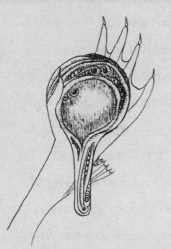 mirror. It was a heavy, beautiful thing, and she could feel the pattern in the silver handle. Even as the fjord spirit reached out to take it, Little Fur opened her mouth to say that Graysong's life had brought the mirror. Then she remembered that this strange, cold creature had tried to save her father—had brought him out of the devouring sea and held him in her arms as he died. Sjoerven took the mirror, but she did not look into it. Her eyes went back to the dead wolves.

"We would give them to the sea, as was the old way," Nightwhisper said. "If you will permit it."

"I will take the true king but not the false," Sjoerven said. Snow began to fall at that moment, as if her coldness had summoned it.

"You must take both or none," Nightwhisper said. "They cannot be separated."

"Then none," said the fjord spirit, and she sank beneath the black water.

"What will happen now?" Gazrak asked.

"It is midwinter night," Little Fur said. "It is time to prepare for the Great Weaving, though I suppose it cannot be so very great when there is only one to weave."

Gem stirred on her shoulder but did not speak. The tiny owl had not spoken since she had bidden Gazrak to offer poison to Graysong.

The two Wolf Kings were left on their pallet as the wolf pack brought enough black rock for a fire to be lit. Watching the flames lick the darkness, Little Fur thought of Tillet and all those who would be in her wilderness now, lighting another fire in the clearing before the seven Old Ones. The fire was dangerous, but its wild power was needed for the weaving.

To Little Fur's surprise, as the night deepened, creatures began to come—wolves and clouded leopards, silver hares and snow birds—all bearing offerings of food. Then came creatures of the past ages: cave dwarfs and gnomes with white mantles of fur, selkies and a small giant, a snow pixie and three weary pine dryads. There were many other sorts of creatures, too, that Little Fur had never seen in the wilderness.

The last to come was the silver fox, No-One. Little Fur greeted her warmly, wondering how all who had come knew it was safe without ever being told.

As the moon set, everyone gathered in a circle about the fire, and the creatures of the last age began to sing, accompanied by the sounds the beasts and birds made. It was not a song they sang, but something much wilder—a great whirl of sound that fetched embers from the fire and cast them up into the darkness. The wind caught the music of their voices and added its own voice. It was quite a different weaving from that which

was shaped by the wilderness, because here it was full of ice and snow and bare stone. But the power of its summoning was just as strong.

After a long time, Little Fur felt the dreams come. She caught and wove those snagged by her voice into dreams of ice and snow. She bound them into the journey she had made from the wilderness to the ice fields. She wove in Gray-song and Balidor, and her love for Ginger and for the wilderness and for the seven Old Ones. She felt others weaving dreams that reflected their own lives, and gradually all of the dreams were joined into a great tapestry.

Then, as a ruddy glow appeared at the horizon, they all sang the weaving into the waiting earth spirit.

Little Fur suddenly sat down, too tired even to stand.

Luckily there was almost nothing to do, for the food that had been brought was already laid out on the snow. Everyone helped themselves to whatever they liked, then they came back to the fire, or sat away from it if the heat was a bother. Once or twice Little Fur saw wolves glance over to the pallet where their two kings lay dusted in snow. She found herself doing the same, wondering whether it would be best to build a cairn of stones to cover them, for there was no possibility of digging a hole in the frozen earth to bury them.

Ginger brought her some cloudberries, and she ate them slowly, grimacing with startled pleasure at their tart deliciousness. Almost all of the creatures of other ages came to speak with her, for none of them had seen her before and they were curious. To her amusement, she found herself telling them of the midwinter weaving that was held in the wilderness as avidly as Crow might have done.

As the day wore on, creatures and beasts began to depart. Even No-One went, though Little Fur had invited her to accompany them down to the crossroads. The fox promised to visit the wilderness in the spring, despite Gem's ominous-sounding insistence that No-One would "learn to love Sorrow" there. Little Fur had been too relieved to hear the owlet speak again to scold her. Only later did she realize what Gem had really been saying.

By nightfall, only Little Fur, Ginger, Gazrak, Gem and the wolves remained by the fjord. They were all very weary and slept for several hours. The wolves lay on the snow in a great furry pile, with Little Fur and Ginger warm in their midst, though Gazrak muttered that he could hardly close his eyes for all the snoring.

❋   ❋   ❋

"Wake," said a soft voice.

Even in her sleep, Little Fur realized it was Gem's beak tickling her ear. She sat up carefully and climbed out from among the wolves.

"What is it?" she asked Gem.

"*She,*" Gem hooted softly. "She comes."

Little Fur and Gem watched as Sjoerven rose from the ice water a third time, her eyes the palest lilac and her hair floating rather than dragging in the black water. She looked at the bodies of Graysong and Balidor for a long time. It seemed to Little Fur that there was a tenderness in her regard.

"Greetings, Sjoerven of the ice," Little Fur said.

The spirit looked at her. "Greetings, Little Fur of the wilderness. Thank you for the mirror."

"You saw what happened?"

The fjord spirit nodded with grief in her eyes. "I did not understand. I will take them both. . . . Perhaps I was at fault. If I had not been angry at Balidor, I would have served him better."

"Why did you give him the mirror?" Little Fur asked.

"Graysong told it. I bade the mirror show Balidor what he wanted to see. I knew that he would not ask to see the truth, and so I knew that his seeings would be incomplete. But I did not know what would come of it." She looked at Graysong with longing and regret. "They live such short lives, the beasts of this age, and no matter how you love them, they cannot stay even if they wish it." She sighed.

"Thank you for telling me about my mother and father," Little Fur said. "I never knew anything about them before."

"I can look into my mirror and tell you more, if you desire it."

Little Fur thought and felt the world around her—the earth, the ice, the air and the living beings. Then she shook her head.

For the first time, the fjord spirit smiled. "You are wise, Little Fur. Now see how Sjoerven honors kings."

There was a *crack* and a loud gnashing of the ice sheet as it broke. The wolves woke and leaped up in alarm. Soon they all stood along the shore gazing at the jagged path that had been opened in the ice that covered the fjord. Floating on it was the pallet upon which lay Graysong and Balidor. Sjoerven reached out and drew it after her. Above her in the sky hung a massive shimmering curtain of blues and greens.

When the pallet was out of sight and the brilliant curtains of light in the sky had vanished, Little Fur, Ginger, Gazrak and Gem bade the wolves farewell and set off for the lowlands.

Three days later, they could see the human high houses rising up in the distance, and the mountains behind were turning to clouds. Little Fur's mind rushed toward the city and the wilderness. She thought of the black dog and Sorrow. How she longed to walk among the Old Ones and feel their spirits about her. And what fun it would be to tell Brownie of all the new creatures she had met at the weaving. And what of Sly? Had she given up her idea of releasing Danger from the zoo?

"You did not ask the fjord spirit what happened to your mother," Ginger said, interrupting the giddy tumble of her thoughts.

Little Fur stroked the elf cloak, clasped the green stone about her neck, and her spirit grew quiet. She shrugged and said, rather shyly, "Perhaps it is not necessary to know everything all at once."

Ginger said nothing, but he purred.

ACKNOWLEDGMENTS

This book was written over hundreds of cups of coffee and croissants and to some incredible French music in the Francouzský Palačinky Restaurace in Prague. The staff was wonderful at the delicate balancing act of looking after me and leaving me alone. I would like to thank Jan and Adelaide, without whose artistic companionship I could never have brought Little Fur to these pages. Thanks also to Janet and Marina, to Nan, and to Ken, Jiri and Peter, for countless random acts of help, guidance and inspiration. And a special, sincere thanks to Mallory Loehr, whose editing teaches me to be a better writer.

ABOUT THE AUTHOR

Isobelle Carmody began the first of her highly acclaimed Obernewtyn Chronicles while she was still in high school, and worked on it while completing a bachelor of arts and then a journalism cadetship. The series and her short stories have established her at the forefront of fantasy writing in Australia.

She has written many award-winning short stories and books for young people. *The Gathering* was a joint winner of the 1993 CBC Book of the Year Award and the 1994 Children's Peace Literature Award. *Billy Thunder and the Night Gate* (published as *Night Gate* in the United States) was short-listed for the Patricia Wrightson Prize for Children's Literature in the 2001 NSW Premier's Literary Awards.

Isobelle divides her time between her homes in Australia and the Czech Republic.

Don't miss Little Fur's next adventure!

Available soon from Yearling

Riddle of Green

Little Fur faces her greatest challenge yet when a confrontation with trolls cuts her off from the flow of earth magic—and from the magical wilderness she calls home. Undertaking a difficult journey in pursuit of the Earth Spirit, Little Fur and Crow are joined by the mad lemur Olfen and a shapeshifter named Danger. Along the way, Little Fur will finally learn the whole truth about her troll mother and elf father. But will she be able to embrace her heritage, when doing so may change the world forever?

Excerpt copyright © 2009 by Isobelle Carmody.
Published by Yearling, an imprint of Random House Children's Books,
a division of Random House, Inc., New York.

CHAPTER 1
The Harling

Trolls were the last thing on Little Fur's mind as she made her way through the human city on her way back home from where the lemmings lived. The white vixen named Nobody and a lemming named Lim accompanied her. It was before dawn on a spring morning, and the air was sweet with new blossoms. Little Fur was pleased to see how many of the seeds she had planted in tiny cracks and crannies had quickened. She thought that even the humans must be able to feel the flow of earth magic, strengthened as it was by all the new growth.

Certainly all the animals in the wilderness were giddy with joy, and the birds were even more scatter-minded than usual. Only the fox called Sorrow was unmoved. Little Fur glanced at the vixen padding along beside her. Nobody had come to the wilderness in the last days of winter, seeking Sorrow, whom she was destined to love. But Sorrow had rejected Nobody, saying that he was an unnatural fox with no true wildness in him, having been raised and used by humans. He swore that he would never take a mate or sire any kits. Sorrow did not care that Nobody's white pelt and lavender eyes had made even her own father call *her* unnatural.

Nobody had not yet spoken of returning to the ice mountains where she had been born, but the lovely scent of hope in her was beginning to fade. Little Fur was sad to think of the two foxes, destined to love one another but living apart. If only she could talk to Sorrow about Nobody . . . but she did not know how to broach his ferocious solitude.

Little Fur sighed and looked up, her eyes searching bits of sky between the buildings for the ragged black shape that was Crow. He was spying out the way ahead as usual, scanning the streets for the furtive movements of greeps. They preferred the dark hours, and the warmth of spring always brought them out of the nooks where they had shivered through the winter.

A small claw plucked at her tunic, and Little Fur looked down to find Lim regarding her with huge, anxious eyes. "The Teta will be well now?" the lemming asked. Lemmings called all of the older females in their clan Teta, but Little Fur knew that Lim meant the prime teta of his clan. The Teta was a very grand personage, despite her diminutive size, and very dignified and stern.

"The Teta is not truly ill," Little Fur explained gently to Lim. "It is only that she is having bad dreams."

"Perhaps the Sett Owl will tell the meaning of the Teta's dreams," Lim said, with the grave, direct courtesy of his kind.

Little Fur had advised the Teta to seek the wisdom of the Sett Owl, though the aged seer was in a trance most days, leaving the monkey Indyk to try to explain any words she spoke. It was odd that the ancient Sett Owl had not given way to her small apprentice, Gem, for she spoke often of the moment when the still magic would release her to join the world's dream. Little Fur thought that perhaps it was time to visit the beaked house again. She could take a tisane to ease the stiff bones and ruined wing of the Sett Owl, and it would be good to see Gem.

"All quietfulness," Crow cawed, swooping low.

The green verge they had been following narrowed to a thin line of grass sprouting between the path and the black road. Little Fur concentrated on stepping along it. She always had to be standing on green and growing things or on good earth in order to connect with the flow of earth magic. Just when the grass ended, at some mossy cobbles, a hissing came from the darkness.

Little Fur stopped and turned to see a sleek black mink poking his sharp snout through a narrow gap between two of the human high houses. His beady eyes fixed upon Little Fur, and he beckoned urgently. Nobody gave a low warning growl, but Little Fur laid a hand on her soft pelt before going toward the lane. The passage was too dark for Little Fur to see far along it, but it was also too narrow to be harboring either human or greep.

"Greetings, Mink," Little Fur said politely.

"Greetings, Not-mink! Greetings!" said the mink, blinking his eyes rapidly. "I have been sent to find you. Sent!"

"One of your brothers is ill?" Little Fur asked, for all minks addressed one another as Brother, whether or not they were male or related.

"It is not-mink who sickens. Not!" the mink hissed. "It is *harling* that is hurt. It reeks of sickness. Is sending this brother mink to find not-mink healer."

"A harling?" said Nobody, pricking her ears. "I thought they had all died out when the age of magic ended."

Little Fur sniffed. There was no stink

of a lie, but minks, like most humans, usually cared only for their own kind. A mink would never seek Little Fur to help another creature unless it had been compelled. This made his story easier to believe, for harlings were said to have the power to impose their will on other creatures.

"Soon the sun will open its eye," Nobody murmured.

"It is not far going! Coming quick quick!" insisted the mink, panting slightly in his agitation. He gestured to the narrow passage behind him, which was clogged with grass and human mess.

Little Fur turned to Lim. "I will go with the mink. You should return to your clan now."

The lemming shook his small head solemnly. "The Teta bade Lim accompany healer to wilderness of Old Ones. Lim must obeying or be dishonored."

Little Fur sighed. There was no way to convince a lemming of anything once it started talking of honor. They were even worse than ferrets!

"Little Fur must waiting! Intrepiditious Crow flying bravely ahead to see what at endfulness of passage," Crow announced. Without waiting for an answer, he circled a high house and disappeared.

"Not goodly to wait!" hissed the mink after a time.

Little Fur looked around anxiously. Crow ought to have returned by now, but the link between them told her that he was safe. No doubt he had stopped to boast about his bravery to some pigeons.

Little Fur nodded. "All right, we will go."

The mink turned and vanished into the passage. Little Fur pushed her water gourd and herb and seed pouches behind her so they would not hamper her movements and pressed through the tangle of growth at the dark, narrow entrance. She could hear the rustling of the mink's progress, and could see the occasional red flash of his eyes as he checked to see if she was following

Little Fur tried to remember what she had heard about the great earth dragons known as harlings. In the age of high magic, they had flown through the ground as swiftly and easily as a bird through the air. When the age of magic ended, they lost their power to transform the earth, and it was said that all the harlings had perished. The thought that one of the legendary creatures might be lying beneath the human city made Little Fur's heart beat faster.

"Mink?" she called softly, for she could no longer smell its scent. "Brother Mink?"

There was no answer.

"He has gone," the vixen said behind her.

"Surely mink is waiting, for he has not yet kept his promise," Lim said earnestly.

Little Fur did not think the mink would abandon them before bringing them to the harling, unless the creature's hold upon him had faltered.

The passage opened onto a small yard covered in thick, soft grass. The yard was surrounded on three sides by the backs of high houses, and on the fourth side by a stone wall partly covered in ivy. In the middle of the yard was a small circular mound built of stone, and half overgrown with ivy as well. No false light shone from any of the looming high houses, but even so, a human glancing out might see her standing there.

Little Fur hurried across the grass and around the mound. On the other side of the mound was a stout arched door with a window in it. A path of crushed white stone led directly from the door to a heavy wooden gate set into the stone wall. Little Fur could smell that humans did not live in the round house, and yet the smell of human was all about it. She was very curious. The round house smelled very old, and humans were always pushing over old dwellings with their road beasts to make way for newer and bigger ones. Yet the neat stone path and short grass told her that humans revered the mound.

From somewhere, a bird uttered a few shrill notes and then fell abruptly silent. Little Fur looked up to see that the sky was turning from indigo to a deep clear blue. There were still a few stars to show it was not quite day. Little Fur knew that if she did not leave the human city now, she would have to hide and wait to return to the wilderness at night.

Nobody was sniffing at a part of the stone wall where the ivy grew thickly. "The mink went over the fence here," she said.

Little Fur nodded. "The harling must have lost its hold on his mind, or —"

"Or it released the mink because he had done what he was sent to do," the vixen murmured. She was sniffing at a scent along the path of crushed stone now, but when she reached the door to the round house, her brush fluffed. "It is open," she said.

Little Fur drew nearer and saw that the bar that ought to have secured the door was propped against the wall and that the door stood slightly ajar. Lim darted forward and slipped through the tiny gap. Little Fur could not follow him, because no earth magic would flow through a solid floor.

She looked anxiously at Nobody, who pushed her nose into the gap to widen it and went through after the lemming.

Little Fur set her hand upon the wall. The moment she touched it, she drew in a breath. Earth magic flowed through the stone! The great age of the dwelling and the lack of humans must have allowed earth magic to reclaim it, Little Fur thought. Then she saw that the round house had no paved floor. The walls rested on good earth. Little Fur stepped inside and was met by a faint, tantalizingly familiar scent, but the sour smell of human that overpowered it was too strong for her to fully make it out.

"Something is under us," Lim said eagerly, his small eyes shining with excitement.

Only then did Little Fur notice that earth magic was pulsing under her feet. She dropped to her knees and pressed her palms to the ground. "It is the harling, but how do I get to it?"

"There might be a way *here*," Nobody said, indicating a fissure running along the floor by the wall. Little Fur saw that there was room enough in the middle for her to wriggle down into it, and her nose told her that the passage widened deeper down. There was a faint scent of troll, too, which told her that the fissure opened onto one of the trollways that led down to Underth.

"I must go down," she said.

"I will come with you," Nobody told her firmly, for she, too, had caught the smell of troll. She turned to Lim. "But someone must guard our backs. Have you the courage to remain here alone and keep watch, Lemming?"

Lim rose up on his hind legs and bowed his assent to the white fox with great dignity. Little Fur squeezed into the crack. She was touched by the way the vixen had ensured the safety of the lemming without wounding his small pride.

Little Fur worked her way down until she reached a narrow path. It ran a short distance, then split in two. She dropped to her knees at the fork and again pressed her palms to the earth. Her heart leapt, for her troll senses told her that the harling was directly under the fork. The crust of earth between the enormous creature and the air was as thin as an eggshell.

"Greetings, Healer." The words were like the distant sound of stones being tumbled in swift-flowing water. Little Fur felt them as a vibration under her feet as much as words in her mind.

"Greetings, Lord of the Earth," she said.

"Lord no more," the harling said wearily, the hissing of sand over stone in its voice. "Better say 'groveling worm,' for I will fly no more."

"You are hurt, Lord," Little Fur said gently. "I will help you. But you will have to tell me what to do, for I have never had the honor of treating one such as you before."

"You cannot help me, unless you will do what you have refused to do."

"Refused?" Little Fur repeated, baffled. "I do not understand."

"The Troll King is ill, but you have refused to help him, though troll blood runs in your veins," answered the harling.

"I did not refuse the Troll King healing, because I did not know he was ill. But if he had summoned me, I would have feared to go to him, for he would rather die than ask for help from one he regards as his enemy."

"Can this be true?" the harling rumbled. "That is not what they told me."

" 'They'?" Little Fur echoed, beginning to be alarmed. She glanced at Nobody and saw that her brush had begun to fluff out with apprehension.

"A trick," the vixen warned, glancing around cautiously.

"Go back to Lim," Little Fur bade her. "Get him away from here."

"What about you?"

"I must see what I can do for the harling," Little Fur answered.

"The harling lured you here," Nobody said.

"He is in pain, and he was deceived," Little Fur told her. "Go to Lim now. I will be able to smell the trolls long before they get here."